THE GIRL
WITH THE
RED
BOOTS

Also by Alex Wheatle

Liccle Bit
Crongton Knights
Straight Outta Crongton
In The Ends
Home Girl

ALEX WHEATLE

THE GIRL WITH THE RED BOOTS

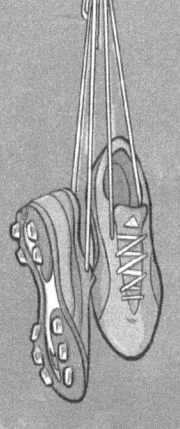

HODDER CHILDREN'S BOOKS

First published in Great Britain in 2025 by Hodder & Stoughton

5 7 9 10 8 6 4

Text copyright © Alex Wheatle, 2025
Cover illustration copyright © Berat Pekmezci, 2025

The moral right of the author has been asserted.

*All characters and events in this publication, other than those clearly
in the public domain, are fictitious and any resemblance to
real persons, living or dead, is purely coincidental.*

All rights reserved.
No part of this publication may be reproduced, stored in
a retrieval system, or transmitted, in any form or by any means, without
the prior permission in writing of the publisher, nor be otherwise circulated
in any form of binding or cover other than that in which it is published
and without a similar condition including this condition being
imposed on the subsequent purchaser.

A CIP catalogue record for this book
is available from the British Library.

ISBN 978 1 444 96966 5

Typeset in Palatino LT Std by Palimpsest Book Production Limited, Falkirk, Stirlingshire

Printed and bound in Great Britain by Clays Ltd, Elcograf S.p.A.

The paper and board used in this book
are made from wood from responsible sources.

Hodder Children's Books
An imprint of
Hachette Children's Group
Part of Hodder & Stoughton Limited
Carmelite House
50 Victoria Embankment
London EC4Y 0DZ

The authorised representative in the EEA is Hachette Ireland, 8 Castlecourt Centre,
Dublin 15, D15 XTP3, Ireland (email: info@hbgi.ie)

An Hachette UK Company
www.hachette.co.uk

www.hachettechildrens.co.uk

I'd like to dedicate this novel to my wife and children, who have cared for me so much since my illness. They have ensured that I have met all my appointments, been there for me when I most needed them and looked out for my every need.

Also, I want to give a big shout-out to all my close friends and extended family, who continue to reach out to check how I'm doing and send their best wishes and flowers. You're all greatly appreciated as I continue to battle my cancer diagnosis.

And to the consultants, nurses and staff at Luton & Dunstable University Hospital, who continue to treat me for my health issues.

One Love to you all.

1

South Street

Mum always told me not to kick my football along the street. 'If a big truck come and squash it, don't bother come running to me!'

It had been a fourteenth birthday gift from my eighteen-year-old brother, Edson. Mum had bought me a mobile phone – she also moaned about my use of that at the dinner table.

On the way home from school, I had always kept close control of the ball. It never escaped my feet. To impress my school friends, I'd play keepy-uppy on the pavement, dribble past pedestrians and play one-twos off walls, trees and fences.

'Me bet you can't do this with your bend-up toe and boomerang feet!' I bragged to my friends.

'You're too boasty!' replied Sienna. 'One day your ball will drop down to the gulley where the mosquito breed.'

It was Friday.

Sienna, Melody and I had finished school for the day. We swaggered down South Street in our green and yellow uniforms. The afternoon sun roasted our head-tops as we swapped banter about boys, trending songs and celebrity gossip. We looked forward to treating ourselves with cool drinks and hot snacks at the Juici Pattie takeaway store.

As we approached Old Harbour town centre, it was the usual hustle and bustle. Impatient drivers blared their horns. Cyclists shouted for more room on the roads. They cussed badwords as drivers ignored them. Mothers yelled at small children to keep to the pavement. Higglers raised their voices at passers-by, still hoping to win a late afternoon sale for their fruits, vegetables and bammy. Minivan and taxi drivers packed their vehicles to the max. Miss Winnie, an old lady, sat in her usual chair at Louis's bar taking her time over her bottle of Dragon Stout. She watched the world go by and listened to the quarrelling car horns.

Suddenly there was another sound.

Crack.

It split the air, echoed and bruised the insides of my ears. I held my ball in my hands and stood still. Sienna and Melody looked ahead towards Old Harbour town square. People ran in all directions. Young children were scooped up in their parents' arms.

South Street

'Get flat!' someone called. 'Get flat! Gunshot!'

A white pick-up truck raced towards us on the wrong side of the road. It blasted its horn as other drivers were forced to swerve to avoid a collision. I almost tripped over as I backed away. The driver of the pick-up wagon had momentarily lost control. His wheels sang a high-pitched tune as they threw up dust on the grass verge. He hurtled towards us. Fear gripped my heart. I felt its beat vibrating inside my throat. Tension stiffened my fingers.

As the driver passed, a rush of wind cooled my face. He caught me in his glare. Hard eyes. Dark skin. Short hair. A thick silver neck chain. A wispy goatee beard. I guessed he was around twenty-one. He owned a crusty build that I imagined could deliver a powerful punch.

I only glanced at it for a short second, but I thought I spotted a gun sitting on the front passenger seat.

He flashed by. *Lord Jesus! Please don't make him turn back.* Other motorists tooted their horns at him, but he was well on his way to the toll road.

The shouts and screams coming from the town centre became clearer.

'Oh, my Lord!' someone cried. 'Dem kill a next one.'

'The boy just stand up so in the queue to get into the bank and get shot up!'

'Me can't believe dem shoot a somebody so close to the police station.'

'Dem have no respect for life!'

'Someone call one-one-zero!'

The Girl With the Red Boots

I shared a look with Melody and Sienna. No one said a word. Instead, we sprinted towards the square to see who had been gunned down.

I couldn't explain it, but I had this creeping dread strangling my heart. It spread to the inside of my stomach. I dashed ahead of my friends and reached the crime scene.

I could just about see through the gathered crowd. Three policemen were in attendance. They were shadowed by the town centre clocktower. One of them spoke into his phone. Another tried to push the throng back. 'Move back! Move back! Give we room.'

The third officer knelt to examine the body. His broad back blocked my view. He raised a hand of the victim and checked a pulse. After a few seconds, he turned round and said to his fellow officer, 'No saving this one.'

I recognised the victim's trainers. Yellow with the Puma green stripe. Blood spattered his three-quarter-length jeans. A deep red soiled the collar of his lime-coloured T-shirt. Something gripped and twisted inside me. A scorching heat blazed through my head. I dropped to my knees as I sensed every vein pulsing in my body. I fell backwards. Sienna caught me. I opened my mouth as I fought for air.

'Noooo! It can't be. Nooooo!'

I'm not quite sure what happened in the following moments. *Did I faint?* I had lost any feeling in my legs. I remembered someone taking my phone.

'What's his name?'

'Edson. Edson Best.'

South Street

'Me know him,' someone said. 'Me watch him play football on Saturdays. Him really good.'

'The gal who drop is his sister.'

'Somebody has to call their mother.'

'Call the father too.'

'Give the gal a drink, mon.'

'Make sure she's sitting comfortably. She just get one mighty shock. Deep trauma she suffering from.'

'Take her away from the scene! She don't need to sight the body.'

'Somebody cover the boy's head. A terrible someting! Nobody need to see that! May our Lord Jesus take care of him.'

'Gunman never meant to shoot the boy. The bullet was intended for somebody else.'

'The Lord God will strike dem down. Evil, dem evil!'

I focused and tried to compose myself.

A gentleman from the nearby bank offered a fold-up chair for me to sit on. My legs wobbled as I took my seat. His white shirt was spotless, and his blue and yellow tie was neatly secured.

'Take time,' he said. 'Take time. Is there anyting else me can do?'

'Me all right.'

I wasn't all right.

Sienna placed a glass of cold water in my hands.

I trembled.

Melody rubbed my back.

'I'll call your mum,' Sienna offered.

I nodded. Or I think I did.

'Miss Claudette.' Sienna spoke into her phone. Her voice was hesitant. 'Miss Claudette.'

There was a long pause.

Sienna thumbed the mobile on speaker. She closed her eyes and tried to control her breathing.

'Sienna? Is that you?' my mother asked.

'Yes . . . yes. Miss Claudette. Me have someting terrible to tell you. Me don't know how . . .'

'Someting terrible?' Mum repeated. 'Kadeen in trouble wid her English teacher again? Me done tell her already to stop the talking back.'

'No . . . it's not that.'

'Then what is it? Is she all right?'

The world stopped as Sienna paused again.

'Someting happened in the square just outside the National Commercial Bank, Miss Claudette.'

'Stop taking the long route, Sienna! Tell me what ah gwaan?'

'It's Edson,' Sienna said.

Silence.

'He's been involved in an accident?' wondered Mum. 'Is he all right? Me always say dem drive too reckless in the middle of town. It's one of dem taxi driver, isn't it? Or one of the minibus men. The police should really do someting about dem.'

'No . . . it's not an accident, Miss Claudette. Somebody shoot him.'

South Street

My brain informed me that Sienna uttered the word *shoot*. My heart refused to believe it.

'Oh, Kadeen,' Sienna said. 'Me just can't believe it. What a tragic loss.'

Maybe it was a mistake? Perhaps she meant someone kicked or punched him. And he's just in a daze. Maybe I'm confused and seeing tings? He'll come round in a minute. Everyting's gonna be OK.

'What do you mean shoot?' asked Mum. Her voice was shaky. It was like she was in denial too.

'I . . .'

Sienna glanced at me and then stared at the ground.

'Somebody shoot Edson,' Sienna continued. 'He's . . . he's not moving.'

'Oh, my God! Is he alive?' Mum wanted to know. 'Is he alive?'

'Me . . . me don't tink so,' Sienna stuttered. Tears flowed down her cheeks.

'Where's Kadeen?' Mum asked. 'Where she there?'

Sienna handed me the phone.

'Hi . . . hi, Mum,' I managed.

'Is it true?' Mum wanted confirmation. 'Kadeen! Can you hear me? Is it true? Talk to me, child!'

'Yes . . . it's true, Mum. Me . . . me tink he was queuing up to get into the bank. Someone said the gunman shot up the wrong person . . .'

'Yes,' a bystander confirmed. 'Me see the intended target take off like him batty catch fire.'

Tears dribbled over my lips and chin. I closed my eyes and tried to will away the dreadful sensation in my stomach. *This can't be.* My mouth felt dry. I simply couldn't continue speaking. In my inner vision, all I could see was the spots of blood on Edson's three-quarter-length jeans and the red stain on his light-green T-shirt.

He was so looking forward to his day. He was going to meet with friends this evening to celebrate someone's new job. They had all worked hard in high school. Edson was on his way to becoming a maths and PE teacher.

Edson's footwear was another birthday gift from Mum. I was there to enjoy his wide grin when he first tried them on.

'These trainers are expensive in Jamaica,' he had said to me. 'Me going to make sure that me worthy of dem.'

Oh, God! This can't be happening. How could The Most High let it happen?

'Kadeen?' Mum said. 'Me coming. Give the phone back to Sienna.'

I found myself trapped in a world between reality and trying to wish away what had happened. The buildings remained the same. I heard the voices around me but couldn't make any sense of it. The police officers went about their work.

This can't be my brother Edson! It can't be. Tomorrow we'll be kicking ball together, and he'll be instructing me to use me left foot more.

I couldn't recall the conversation between Mum and

South Street

Sienna, and I can't remember how an hour or two later I happened to be in an interview room with two police officers and Mum.

We were on the second floor. The white rotor fan suspended from the ceiling had its own soft rhythm. It cooled the top of my head. Through the windows, I heard the angry traffic outside. A fly crawled up the wall before it buzzed around again. I followed its flightpath and felt a bit dizzy.

A policeman stood by the door with his arms folded, and a female officer sat opposite me. She had short hair under her black hat. She wore a light-blue short-sleeve shirt and black red-striped trousers. Her black shoes shone brightly. Her eyes were full of compassion. I wondered how many dead young men like Edson she had seen in her career. Mum was parked to my left. She pressed her handbag to her stomach as if she had the world's secrets inside it.

There was a small square table between me and the policewoman. Three glasses of water rested on it. I hadn't touched mine. The policewoman smiled and introduced herself.

'I'm Officer Crystal Myers, and my colleague is Officer Clive Hibbert.'

'Good afternoon,' I replied.

Mum nodded.

'I understand that you're divorced, and your ex-husband, Mr Hubert Best, lives in Montego Bay,' said Crystal Myers.

'Yes,' Mum replied.

'Do you want us to inform him of this . . . dreadful news?'

Mum thought about it.

'No,' she replied. 'It's something . . . something me have to do meself.'

'Are you sure?' Crystal wanted confirmation.

'Yes, me sure,' Mum replied.

'Are . . . are you sure you want to be interviewed *today*?' Crystal turned to me. 'We realise this has been a devastating shock for you. Collecting any evidence is a matter of urgency in any homicide, but we can wait until whenever you're ready.'

'We're ready,' Mum replied. 'We want you to catch whoever did this to me son as quickly as possible.'

'And you, Kadeen?' Crystal searched my eyes. 'How do you feel? Are you up to being interviewed about the events leading up to . . . Are you OK to speak with us today? Anything you witnessed may help us.'

Truth was me could barely breathe. I wanted to go back to the start of the day. When everything was normal. Edson had challenged me that if I beat his record of one hundred and eighteen keepie-uppies, he'd take me to Juici Pattie's and me could order whatever me want.

'Not . . . not sure,' I said. 'Me still can't believe it.'

'If you want, I can call someone to escort you home. We can do this another time.'

'No, I'll be all right,' I lied. 'Me want whoever killed my brother to be taken off the streets quick-time.'

'Are you prepared to go through the events from when you left school?' Crystal asked.

I swapped a long look with Mum. She nodded.

'Yes, me tink me can do that.'

Crystal pulled out a small notepad and pen from her breast pocket. 'In your own time,' she said. 'Pause when you need to.'

'We were on our way to Juici Pattie when we heard a gunshot,' I started. 'That's our usual hangout after school. Somebody shouted to get flat. Nuff people drop to the ground. Others ran all over the place. Me and my friends went to see what happened.'

'And Kadeen knows she shouldn't have done that,' interrupted Mum. She turned to me and set her hard glare on me. 'What's wrong wid you, child? You don't run *into* danger.'

'Following the gunshot,' Crystal resumed. 'Did you witness anything out of the ordinary?'

In my mind's eye I could see the white vehicle motoring towards me.

'Yes,' I replied. 'Me see a white pick-up truck – a liccle rusty small one. It was driving on the wrong side of the road. Its horn was blaring. Some other driver cuss badword.'

'Can you confirm that you witnessed this following the gunshot?'

'Yes.' I nodded.

'How long do you think between the gunshot till when you saw the white pick-up truck?'

The Girl With the Red Boots

'About . . . fifteen, maybe thirty seconds. It was very quick.'

Crystal scribbled something down in her notepad.

'Did you recognise the driver?'

I don't think I would ever forget his face.

'Yes, me see him, but me don't tink me ever see him before. He was dark-skinned. He looked kinda stocky, you know, broad-like. Thick arms. He had a goatee beard and short hair. He wore a thick silver chain around his neck.'

'Did you notice anything else? Anything particular about the face?'

Was it a gun resting on the passenger seat? Me not too sure. It might have been someting else. What else could it be? There wasn't anyting me remember in particular about his face, but me wonder if he will recognise my own?

'Me . . . me tink.'

I closed my eyes as I remembered the man's hard stare.

'Yes, go on,' said Crystal.

'Me tink me saw a gun on the front passenger seat,' I said.

'Are you sure?'

I thought about it.

'Me sure it looked like a gun . . . unless me eyes are fooling me. He was going fast but he had his windows open.'

Crystal penned a few more words before she held my gaze again. 'Did you happen to catch the licence plate?'

'No,' I replied. 'Me never tink about that.'

'Is there anything else you can add that may help us with our investigation?'

I closed my eyes and recalled the horrific moment when I realised it was Edson lying still in the town centre square. A pool of blood had collected around his head like a red halo. All my strength had been taken out of me. I still didn't know how I'd managed to walk to the police station.

I couldn't stop the tears. I felt Mum's arm around my shoulders.

'We'll stop there,' Crystal said. 'We'll catch him, I can assure you of that.'

'Me hope so,' said Mum. 'Too much gunman in Jamaica. Where do they get dem from? They don't make guns in this island.'

We were led downstairs to the forecourt where Mum had parked. I climbed into the front passenger seat. Crystal closed the door for me. 'One of our officers will lead you home,' she said.

'Thank you,' replied Mum.

I thought about Dad. He's living and working his normal day. *Oh, Lord!*

2

Marlie Mount

Mum didn't utter a word on the journey home to our Marlie Mount neighbourhood. Instead, she stared so intensely through the windscreen I thought she might bore a hole in it. When we arrived, Mum didn't change into casual clothes like she usually did. She sat on the sofa in the lounge with her eyes closed, twirling her mobile phone in her hands.

'Are you OK, Mum?'

No response.

The paintings hanging on the walls, the flat-screen TV, the grey-black marble flooring, the kidney-shaped coffee table and our open-plan kitchen all looked the same. But it wasn't. I couldn't bring myself to glance in the direction of Edson's room. *I'd never hear him lift weights again at 5.30 a.m.*

Maybe Mum was thinking what I was thinking. *How can we even begin to tell family and friends what happened?*

'I'll . . . I'll start dinner,' I offered.

I'm not sure if Mum heard me. She planted her feet on the coffee table and scrolled the contact list on her mobile. Her fingers hovered over the keypad.

I tried my very best to rid my mind of the image of Edson's lifeless body in the town square.

I just couldn't.

If I wanted to, I could've seasoned the chicken legs with my tears as well as the garlic, spring onions, curry powder and pepper.

I heard Mum's ringtone.

'Yes, I'll be there,' said Mum after a while. 'Soon come.'

She came into the kitchen and hugged me. She then cradled my cheeks as she addressed me.

'I've been asked to identify Edson's body,' she said. 'At Spanish Town Hospital. They said they have . . . made him look presentable.'

'Me will go wid you,' I offered.

'No,' Mum replied. 'You have been through enough trauma for the day. It's someting me have to do.'

'But me want to be wid you to support you.'

'You are supporting me by starting dinner. I'll be back as soon as I can.'

'Shall me start calling family?' I offered. 'And what about Dad? He needs to know.'

Mum pressed her lips together. She squinted. 'I'll call

him when I get back,' she said. 'Me don't want you stressing yourself ringing everybody. You're only fourteen, Kadeen. There are some tings that a parent has to do.'

Mum still hadn't changed. She drove to the hospital in her cream-coloured trouser suit. Her high-heeled sandals niced up her feet. Working as a receptionist at TV Jamaica, she was expected to look smart and respectable. It didn't seem appropriate to identify Edson's body dressed like that. *What is appropriate? I hope they have cleaned the . . . from his face.*

Twenty minutes later, Sienna called, wondering if she should come over to give me support. When we parted ways at the square, she was crying more than I was.

'Maybe later,' I said. 'When Mum gets back, we have to start calling family.'

'OK, me understand.'

There was leftover sweet potato, yams and spinach in the fridge that I could heat up in the microwave to add to the chicken when Mum got home. She always insisted that we eat our evening meal together. *But Edson's gone. He'll never fill his chair again. I'd never hear him calling me Liccle Miss Messi. He'll no longer enter me bedroom and salute my Khadija Shaw poster over my bed. No more will he tickle my foot-bottom when I oversleep on a school morning.*

'Yes, you can dribble around trees and lampposts,' he'd say. 'But trees and lampposts can't tackle. And use your left foot more.'

Then he'd laugh that belly laugh of his, creasing his eye-corners.

It got all too much for me. I called Sienna and she came round to help me finish the chicken.

Mum returned an hour and a half later. She looked broken.

I served her dinner, and she hardly ate anything. Instead, she fiddled with her fork and stared out through the window at the side of the house. I didn't think our lime tree had any answers. I pictured Edson squeezing lime juice into a glass.

Sienna and I didn't know what to say to support her.

'Are we going to call Dad?' I suggested. 'And the rest of the family? They need to know. If you want, I can start calling my cousins?'

'Don't you have homework to do, Kadeen?' Mum raised her voice. 'Last night you were working on a history assignment – have you finished it yet? And instead of kicking that damn football of yours when you're out and about tomorrow I want you to do some shopping. And I have to arrange for a temp to cover for me at the TV station.'

'Mum . . .'

'And I don't want to hear that you're talking back to your English teacher again. Do you hear me, Kadeen? Respect your teachers!'

Sienna and I swapped a concerned glance. I stood up slowly. 'Mum, me don't tink I'll be going to school on Monday, or for the rest of the week. We must start arranging tings, contacting family.'

Mum dropped her head. She covered her face with her

palms. I watched her for a short while. I wasn't sure if she remained in that position for three minutes or ten. 'We must carry on,' she said finally. 'We can't let people down.'

'Mum!' I shouted. 'Edson's gone . . . we can't carry on as normal. We're not letting anyone down.'

Mum raised her head and wiped her face. She desperately tried to stem her tears, but eye-water ran down her cheeks. Her lips wobbled. I had never seen her like this before, not even when Gran died. Guilt licked me for raising my voice. I moved quick to wrap an arm around her.

'We'll . . . we'll do it together,' I said. 'Family has to be told.'

'I'll help,' offered Sienna.

An hour later, Mum finished her conversation with Dad. It's good that they still had a fine working relationship even though they were divorced. 'He wants to speak with you,' she said.

I picked up the phone and gave myself a moment. I took a deep breath.

'How . . . how are you holding up?' he asked.

'Me . . . me not sure what that means, Dad. Me sight Edson lying on the ground, but it was like it wasn't him. He wasn't there. Me can't explain it. Like his spirit had left his body. Me still can't believe he's gone. Me thinking he'll walk in at any second cracking his jokes.'

'Do you want me to come round?'

'Maybe tomorrow,' I replied. 'We still have so many people to contact.'

'Me really don't mind making the drive.'

'Dad, you live in Montego Bay. It'll take you, what? At least an hour and a half. Maybe two.'

'He was coming up to stay wid us next week.'

'Yes, me know.'

A long silence. Then I heard a sniffle.

Is Dad crying? It's hard for him too.

'Is there anyting else me can do?'

'Can't tink of anyting right now,' I said. 'Just do what Mum asked, you know, call the undertakers.'

'The undertakers,' Dad repeated. 'Yes, I'll do that first ting in the morning. Then I'll drive down to see you.'

'Thank you, Dad.'

'Love you, Kadeen.'

'Love you too, Dad.'

'Oh . . . how is Simone?'

'She's fine,' Dad replied. 'She's learning her ABCs. She's a bright little ting with a whole heap of energy.'

'I'll look forward to seeing her next time me come up . . . oh, and Monica too.'

'We look forward to having you.'

I killed the call and burst into tears.

Undertakers.

I couldn't spot my football anywhere. I frantically searched for it around the house and in the garden but was unable to find it.

'Where is it? Where is it?'

Tears came to my eyes once again.

'In the boot,' Mum replied, breaking off from a phone conversation.

Relief.

I collected my ball from Mum's car and continued to ring relatives and family friends. Aunt Doreen was dramatic.

'Is what kinda madness yuh telling me, Kadeen? Lord give you strength! Evil, dem ah evil. May God comfort your sweet mama and guide you. God bless you, chile.'

I was so grateful to Sienna. She stayed with us for the rest of the night.

Time dragged on to 3 a.m. and I just couldn't sleep. Nor could the crickets and cicadas, who argued outside.

I crept into Edson's room, half expecting to see him sprawled across his bed. I switched on the light, and I found everything was in place. Books were neatly stacked on their bookshelf. His pens and pencils had their own jar on his desk beside his textbook on twenty-first-century Caribbean economies. Post-it stickers decorated his laptop. His weights were neatly arranged underneath the window. His selection of baseball hats filled a long shelf. His footwear was tidily placed against the opposite wall, and his bed was made so well it could've been in a furniture showroom in New Kingston.

Posters of LeBron James, Kylian Mbappé and Coco Gauff watched over everything.

'Watch me!' he had said to me recently. 'One day me going to teach at Harvard or Stanford.'

I had to get out before I collapsed.

Marlie Mount

I went outside with my ball, and repeatedly kicked it against the side of my house.

Usually, Mum would cuss badword. This time she said nothing.

3

Identification

Edson's funeral had taken place at Dovecot Memorial Park near Spanish Town. There wasn't a cloud in the sky, and I believed it was God's way of making my brother's rise to heaven free and easy. It was only when his coffin was lowered into the ground that I broke down. He was buried in his Inter Miami Lionel Messi shirt, his Jamaican football shorts and his yellow and green trainers. Mum had carefully placed his calculator in his hands – he had had it since his first day of high school.

The minister assured the congregation that *Edson's in God's company, and He'll take great care of him.*

I didn't want God to have him.

God's too damn greedy. Why does He take all the good ones?

Dad, Sienna and Melody tried their best to comfort me,

Identification

but I simply couldn't bear the pain. I wanted to tell Edson that he was the best big brother a girl could ever wish for. But I couldn't. *He's in the ground. Forever.*

All because of some reckless guy who thinks he's a man becah he had a gun. Didn't he have a small grain of thought that when he aimed his firearm, an innocent bystander could be shot? Didn't he tink about that? Wherever he is, is he tinking about Edson right now? Can he imagine what it feels like to bury someone you love, so young, who hasn't done anyting wrong? Who had his whole life in front of him? Doesn't he feel a tiny dose of guilt?

Me feel sick. Me don't tink me can keep anyting down today.

What are the police doing in their investigation? Since my interview at the station, we hadn't heard from them. It's been three weeks. This broad-chested, reckless killer is still out there somewhere. Do they care?

The rest of the day went by in a blur. Various relatives, school and college friends of Edson, some who I remembered and others I did not, offered kind words and hugs.

'When you're ready, Kadeen, come look for we. Too long me nuh see you.'

People attended from Mum's TV station. I recognised three newsreaders, the sports correspondent and the pretty weather girl. They all invited me to visit the station for work experience, but I didn't even want to return to school.

My Aunt Doreen looked after the cooking for the wake. Mum's brother, Uncle Bukkus, poured the drinks, and wasn't shy about serving himself. 'A terrible, terrible someting! Edson was a good boy. Me hear that he was very good at football. The Most High take the very good people young.'

There were long speeches, even longer tears, and raised glasses. I couldn't understand why guests stayed so late. Uncle Phillip didn't leave until after 2 a.m. I understood that many relatives hadn't seen each other for a while and they were catching up, but I just wanted to be left alone to grieve in peace.

Two days later, Officer Crystal Myers came by with one of those artist portfolio cases. Mum offered Crystal a mixed juice drink with crushed ice as she cleared the coffee table and placed her case on it. I was in my room, scrolling through all the pictures of Edson on my phone, when Mum called me in. I made my way to the lounge.

Crystal unzipped the portfolio as Mum poured the drinks. It contained a set of black-and-white laminated photographs. I guessed they were ten inch by eight in size.

'Now, Kadeen, take your time,' Crystal said. 'If any of these men look like the man making his getaway in the white pick-up truck, please let me know.'

She flipped the images over. The first one was a brown-skin brother with close-set eyebrows. He had a square jaw and an intense gaze. *Not him.*

The second pic was a slim-faced, dark-skinned man with a skinny moustache. He had a tiny gold cross stuck in his left ear. *Not him.*

Identification

The third image was of a mix-race man with green eyes and a full beard. I shook my head.

What stupidness are they thinking? I made it clear in my interview – the man was dark-skinned with short hair and a wispy goatee beard.

Officer Myers turned over the next photo.

Jesus cripes!

My back stiffened as something cold jellyfished around my spine and weaved between my ribs.

There he was. Hard, shark-like eyes. He had a small scar beneath his left eye. His cheeks looked like his mum pinched them nuff times when he was a kid. He didn't have his goatee in the picture, but it was definitely him.

I nodded and side-eyed Crystal.

'Are you sure?' Crystal pushed me.

'Yes, me sure.'

Crystal and Mum shared a knowing look.

'What is it?' I asked.

'Can . . . can I speak to your mum in private?' Crystal asked.

'Why?' I wanted to know. 'Is it about the man who me just identified?'

'Kadeen,' Mum called. 'Just go to your room for two minutes. *Please.*'

I offered Mum and Crystal a cold eye-pass before I stepped away.

My football sat at the foot of my unmade bed. Jamaican football hero Khadija Shaw stared down at me. Commiseration cards filled my corner desk and my bookshelves. The largest one was from my PE teacher, Ms Lannaman. She knew my favourite colour because she had pinned a red rose to it. Team members from football, cricket, basketball and athletics had all signed it. I even received a card from Miss Bradley, my English teacher – she had beautiful handwriting.

We're all here praying for you, Kadeen.
Edson was much loved at our school and so are you.

Lionel Messi's biography sat next to my pillow. Edson bought me the book to make up for spraining my ankle in a tackle a few weeks ago.
Edson is everywhere in this house.
I picked up my ball and played keepy-uppy with it until I lost control.
'Kadeen!' Mum yelled. 'No kicking the ball in the house. How many times me have to tell you!'
I left my room and went outside. Mum didn't holler at me as I booted my ball against the side of the house. Two hundred kicks later, she beckoned me in.
She hugged me and stroked my hair before I sat down in the lounge. Her half-smile couldn't disguise the worry groove in her forehead. The single grey strand she had in her hair seemed to lengthen. She couldn't hide the fear in her eyes.
Crystal cleared her throat before she spoke. 'I was

Identification

advising your mum that, as a precaution, you might want to consider moving away from Old Harbour as we continue this investigation.'

'Move away?' I repeated. 'Why?'

Mum and Crystal shared a quick look.

'The man you identified has been wanted by the police for a long time.'

'For what?'

Crystal swallowed. Her throat danced. She gave herself a second. 'Suspicion of murder,' she revealed.

'Two murders,' added Mum.

The icy slithering returned to my bones.

'He's a member of a notorious gang that has contacts not just in Jamaica and the Caribbean,' Crystal continued, 'but in Central America too.'

My legs felt strange. My toes tingled.

'So . . .' I managed. 'What you telling me? We're . . . we're not safe?'

'As I say, it's a precaution,' Crystal assured me. 'Only my colleagues know who we have interviewed in this investigation. That information is strictly confidential.'

'But Edson's murder was reported in the newspapers,' Mum said. 'His full name was printed. It was on the front page of *The Star* – drive-by shooting in big loud letters.'

'Mum? Mum? Will he come after us?'

Mum switched her hard gaze on to Crystal. Crystal fidgeted in her chair. 'As I said, we're suggesting moving away from Old Harbour just as a precaution. Better to be safe than sorry. Do you have anywhere else to stay? Family maybe? Friends?'

'My sister, Doreen, is in May Pen, and I have a brother, Bukkus, who lives in Mandeville,' Mum replied. 'And another brother, Phillip, in Port Antonio.'

'My dad lives in Montego Bay,' I said.

Mum stared at me hard before she turned to Crystal. 'We both can't stay in Montego Bay,' she said. 'My ex-husband now has a new wife, and . . .'

'I understand,' nodded Crystal.

'What about Kadeen's education?' Mum asked.

'To be safe, it might be an idea for Kadeen to attend another school,' suggested Crystal. 'We have put more officers on the street, and there'll be a few more patrolling the school area. We want the community to feel safe. But we don't want witnesses walking about central Old Harbour. Better safe than—'

'Sorry,' I finished.

'But you said yourself,' Mum raised her tone, 'this gang has contacts all over Jamaica and Central America. Can she really be safe inna Jamaica?'

'Maybe Sienna or Melody can bring me work from school?' I suggested.

Mum shook her head. 'They might need to take precautions too. We can't have dem coming up to the yard.'

'That is true,' Crystal agreed. 'Both of dem have made statements.'

'Then what?' I asked.

Identification

'Aunt Mel,' replied Mum.

'She lives in England,' I said. 'That place has broad shiny buildings and even broader grey clouds. And it's too damn cold.'

'But safe,' added Mum.

'And Aunt Mel's too strict,' I argued. 'In a previous life, me sure she was a sergeant in the army. When we went to stay wid her, she wouldn't even let me go to the Notting Hill Carnival.'

'You were only twelve years old,' said Mum. 'We weren't about to have you gallivanting on street at that age.'

'Children younger than me went,' I protested. 'They sprayed up dem face wid paint and dance 'pon the streets without a worry in the world.'

'*Kadeen!*' Mum raised her voice. 'Right now, London is the safest place for you. Me don't want no argument. Me have enough stress 'pon me mind.'

'And she kicked up a whole heap of noise when me play football in the park,' I went on.

'Hold your tongue,' Mum warned. 'You didn't know dem boys from Adam and Eve.'

'Me was just kicking some ball. What's wrong wid that?'

'Er . . . I will leave the decision with you,' cut in Crystal. 'It's my duty to inform you that the individual who you identified is extremely dangerous. He's not to be approached by members of the public under any circumstances.'

'What's his name?' I wanted to know.

The Girl With the Red Boots

I didn't like the way Crystal and Mum swapped another glance.

'His street name is Tony Buttons,' Crystal replied. 'His birth name is Antonio Silva. He was born in Cuba. He's twenty-nine years old according to his Cuban passport, but he may be travelling on another.'

'And he's already a suspect for murder?' I asked.

'A suspect for *two* murders,' Mum corrected. 'That's why I want you to go to Aunt Mel in England.'

'I'm *not* going to England,' I insisted. 'Me have no friends there, the sea is a nasty brown colour and the food don't taste right. Let me go to Dad's.'

'I'll . . . I'll leave you to it,' Crystal said. 'If there are any more developments, I'll let you know as soon as I can.'

Mum showed Crystal to the door. When she returned to the lounge, she hit me with a serious glare. 'Kadeen, you know it'll be . . . awkward if we stay wid your father.'

'Him have a spare room,' I said. 'With an en suite.'

Mum gave me one of her looks.

'I'm *not* going to England,' I repeated as I hot-stepped to my room.

4

Unanimous Decision

The next afternoon, Dad came round.

He was still wearing his work clothes with his belt of tools strapped around his waist. A short pencil was wedged behind his ear, and his black baseball cap covered his bald patch.

In the garage, he dropped his tool-belt and pulled off his boots. It was strange watching him walk barefoot along the marble flooring that he had laid down.

I fixed him a homemade lime juice drink with ice cubes as he settled into an armchair in our lounge. He let out a satisfying sigh as he enjoyed his first sip.

'How's work?' I asked.

'I spent most of my morning trying to tell a man that his corrugated roof won't hold sun panels, but he wanted me to try it anyway. Everybody trying to save money off their electric bill these days.'

Mum joined us and sat on the sofa close to me. She crossed her legs, locked her fingers together and smiled with just her eyes. I felt the tension between my parents.

'Hubert,' Mum greeted. 'How's tings?'

'Not too bad,' Dad replied. 'Can't complain. Work picking up. Me never been so busy.'

'That's good to hear,' said Mum politely. 'How's the wife?'

'Her name is Monica,' Dad reminded. 'She's fine. She'll be starting work again at one of the hotels when we find somebody appropriate to babysit Simone.'

'That's good, that's good. How is Simone?'

'Me was just telling Kadeen that she's learning her ABCs.'

'That's nice.' Mum nodded. 'Now, Hubert, me ask you here today to help explain to Kadeen why she must go to England until they find this bad-breed, no-good-for-nothing Tony Buttons.'

Dad swirled the ice in his glass as he gave himself a moment. He side-eyed me before he spoke.

I cut him off before he began. 'Me know it's kinda awkward for Mum, but me can stay wid you, right?'

Dad hesitated.

'Me have a few friends in Montego Bay,' I added. 'And me liccle sister, Simone. It'll be nice to spend time wid her.'

Dad stared at the floor.

'Dad?' I repeated. '*Don't* tell me I can't stay wid you.'

'This . . . this Tony Buttons,' Dad said. He lifted his head.

Unanimous Decision

'Him well dangerous. He's wanted in Belize as well as Jamaica. They say he's a gun trafficker who has no respect for life. You can't mess wid dem people.'

'But him don't know me have a dad who lives in Montego Bay,' I argued.

'Me . . . me wid your mum on this one,' said Dad. 'Best for you to fly to Aunt Mel. Safe and outta danger.'

'If it's best for me, then why don't Mum come wid me to England?'

'Me wasn't a witness,' replied Mum. 'Me didn't identify Tony Buttons.'

'Tony Buttons don't know that!'

'Me not staying here so,' said Mum. 'As soon as you're gone, me going to stay with Aunt Doreen. She will chat off me ears with her this and that, complain about me cooking, but me must make that sacrifice. The police promised me that they will check on our place every day.'

'So me don't have any choice?'

'We're just trying to keep you safe, Kadeen,' said Dad. 'You don't see that?'

'All me see is this terrorist Tony Buttons killing me brother and dictating where me should rest me head at night-time! Why the police don't catch him yet? Him kill Edson in broad daylight. Nuff people in the square must have seen it.'

'Some people don't want to speak to the police,' replied Dad. 'Dem afraid. You know how it go.'

'The police are doing all they can,' said Mum. 'Hopefully

they'll catch him quick-time, and everyting can go back to normal.'

'Normal?' I repeated. 'Tings can never be normal again.'

'As normal as tings can be,' Mum added.

'It's February,' I said. 'And from what me hear from Aunt Mel, England cold like the North Pole at this time of year. The sun is a stranger in that part of the world. Even polar bear want to wear a thick coat there.'

'Kadeen,' Mum said. 'You love to exaggerate too much. The cold is not that bad. Not as bad as a winter in New York.'

'She's going to need winter clothes,' said Dad.

'And me don't want no granny cardigan or old-woman rubber boot to wear,' I said.

'We'll send Aunt Mel a liccle money for winter garments,' promised Mum.

'Why can't you just give me the money? Aunt Mel dress up like she raving in the 1950s. Me know what to buy for myself.'

'Why me don't give you the money?' repeated Mum. 'Becah you might spend it on foolishness. The last time me give you a liccle someting to spend in New Kingston, you waste it on your nails, perfume and takeaway food. London has too many shops to fling away good money.'

'So you're sending me to the coldest, greyest country inna the world and you refuse to even give me a liccle money to buy me own clothes? And you say you love me. *Which part?* You don't trust me?'

Mum narrowed her eyes. She spoke softly and slowly.

'Don't make me take out the big-daddy pliers from the garage to pluck out your feisty tongue.'

I glanced at Dad, but he didn't intervene.

5

Long Goodbyes

Sienna lived about a ten-minute walk away in a bungalow near the old railway track. No one could tell me exactly why the trains had stopped running many years ago. Old people in our community, including my gran, described the carriages like they were part of the Orient Express, and that they sped you to Kingston in ten minutes.

I loved visiting Sienna because there were plenty green spaces between people's homes. Her mum, Glenice, grew colourful flowers around her place, and she had two mango trees in her back garden. I always brought my ball to her neighbourhood, formed goalposts with our school bags and persuaded Melody to go in goal.

'If the ball comes to me direct, I'll save it,' Melody said. 'But me won't dive 'pon hard ground for it and mash up me kneecap!'

Long Goodbyes

It was my last afternoon before I flew to London. Glenice had treated us with Kentucky Fried Chicken. We feasted on chicken legs, fries, barbecue beans and hot wings on the veranda, and chased it down with my fave smoothie, blackberry, mango, banana and strawberry. When I had drained my glass, I picked up my ball and made towards the field.

'Me too full,' protested Melody. 'Me can't dive around wid a full stomach.'

'You never dive around anyway,' I said. 'Come, it's the last time we'll play ball for a long time.'

'Me too tired,' protested Sienna. 'Can't you just kick your ball against the side of the house?'

'It's me last day before me fly out to Greyland,' I said. 'And me two best friend can't play ball wid me?'

'Kadeen, sit down and rest yourself,' said Melody. 'If you start move, the chicken you just eat might want to come back outta your mout'.'

Frustrated, I returned to the veranda.

'How . . . how long do you think you'll be gone?' Sienna asked.

'Till they find this devil pickney Tony Buttons,' I replied. 'Everybody say him a bad mon, wanted for whole heap of murder. Me hope him serve three hundred years in solitary confinement. Me hope that there's plenty big rat in him cell. Me hope him never taste Kentucky Fried Chicken or a juici pattie again.'

'Some say him kill six,' said Melody. 'Me brother say him

part of the Terminator crew. They have been blamed for killing a government minister in Belize. Deadly, dem is deadly.'

'You're flying away at the wrong time,' said Sienna.

'Why you say that?' I asked.

'Becah Cass Buckley won't be single forever,' Sienna replied. 'Don't tink me never notice how you slow down your walking whenever you approach him in the school corridor.'

'Me sight that too,' added Melody. 'You have the love bug bad, Kadeen. Me surprise you don't try to eat him rather than your school dinner.'

'Me not interested in Cass Buckley,' I protested. 'Him two year older than me, and him don't play football.'

'Him run like the October winds though,' said Sienna. 'Ms Lannaman confident he will run for Jamaica one day. Four hundred metres him distance.'

'And him play good basketball too,' added Melody. 'If you have babies for him, they'll be sporty wid nuff stamina, football feet and a fast mout' wid the teachers.'

I spun the ball in my hands. I hoped they'd change the subject.

'You're not interested in Cass?' Sienna teased. 'If me believe that, you might as well tell me that Usain Bolt is short and Jamaica never like reggae.'

'Did you say goodbye to him?' Melody asked. 'Or send him a love letter?'

I stared at the ground. I hoped my infatuation didn't show itself on my face.

Long Goodbyes

'Me don't have him number,' I said. 'Or know where him live.'

'We can go around to his yard,' suggested Sienna. She had a mischievous grin growing from her lips. 'Yes, him don't live too far from here.'

'Tell him what he means to you before you go to England,' urged Melody.

'Forward to his yard?' I protested. 'You tink me crazy? And what do you expect me to say to him?'

'Tell him that you been in love wid him for more than two year,' laughed Sienna. 'And before you rest your eyes at night-time, you tink of him.'

'And he's in your head the first second you wake up,' added Melody.

I threw my ball at Sienna, hitting her on the shoulder. 'You tink me want to bring great shame 'pon myself? Me don't hunt down any man. Better dem come for me.'

'And if you wait too long,' Sienna said, 'before you know it, a good man will be married to the girl next door pushing two pickney in a buggy.'

'Don't worry, Kadeen,' grinned Melody. 'If me sight a next girl making a play for him, I'll push her down the gulley.'

'You would do that for me?' I joked.

'Of course,' grinned Melody. 'If you come back and don't get to flex with Cass, you'll be miserable company.'

'That's no lie,' nodded Sienna. 'Sadness will lick you so hard you'll even stop kicking your ball.'

It suddenly hit me that I had no idea when I would see my friends again.

Who am I going to banter with in England?

'Me going to miss you to the max,' I admitted.

Melody and Sienna stretched out their arms and we enjoyed a group hug. I couldn't stop the tears falling down my cheeks.

'Me going to miss you too,' said Sienna. 'But at least me don't have to play ball wid you for the time being. You're too good.'

'Yes.' Melody nodded. 'She not lying. When you go to England you should play in a proper team and win plenty trophy.'

'Me don't even tink about that,' I replied. 'Me don't believe me Aunt Mel will ever let me play ball. She might even chain me up inna the yard and drop me red football boots down a well.'

'Aunt Mel that bad?' Sienna wanted confirmation.

'Yes, tink of that mad woman in pink in the Harry Potter films and double the strictness.'

'Really?' asked Melody.

'Yes,' I replied. 'One time, when me was nine years old inna England, she take me to a place called Borough Market. It was near London Bridge. Nuff foods from all over the world you could buy there. Plenty people all about. For a liccle while, maybe a minute or so, we lost touch. When she grab me hand again, she tell me I must never wander off again, ever. And if me do, she would slap three sides of my head, and then box me some more. She was serious.'

'She sound like me Uncle Jonathan who lives in Canada,' said Sienna. 'Whenever me was out wid him he would fret and double fret. *Keep close. Always keep in touching distance.'*

'They're just being protective,' said Melody. 'Remember, you're in a foreign country. We know Jamaica. Well, most of it. We know Old Harbour, the Bay and surrounding areas.'

'Talking of the Bay, you're going to miss me birthday treat,' said Sienna. 'Me parents are taking me up to Shelly's Place on the Bay. Dad says they serve the best fish in the island.'

'Shelly's Place!' I repeated. 'Me mum carry us there to celebrate Edson passing his exams. Me had the roasted jackfish with pepper, spring onions and rice. Me belly well satisfy. Me sleep good that night, me tell you.'

A sudden sorrow kicked me hard. I tried my best to compose myself.

Edson loved his food. Especially roasted fish. On that birthday evening, he took me to the beach and taught me this new dance to an Afrobeat. I had football feet, and I couldn't quite follow all the moves. But Edson always had patience with me. 'Step to the right, then to the right again, and drop to your left before you step to your right once more. You'll get it, Kadeen. Just practise.'

'As we sample some fresh tender fish,' Melody smiled, 'and look out to the calm sea beneath the setting pink sun as our toes sink into the sand, we'll tink of you in cold Greyland.'

'And the next morning we'll take a walk along the Bay beach and watch the fishermen paddle their boats to the ocean.'

'Don't come back if you catch nothing.' Sienna raised her voice. 'So their women tell dem before they disappear.'

I stared at the ground and pushed back my tears. 'Me still don't want to go to England,' I said.

'Don't worry,' replied Sienna. 'You'll be back before you can dream of Cass Buckley's abs and long legs. And you better bring me back a birthday present from England.'

'Are you taking your ball?' asked Melody.

'Of course!' I said. 'Me can't leave it behind. Edson buy it for me. Aunt Mel must go to work – that'll be my ball time. Me bringing me red boots too! Edson buy me dem for Christmas.'

'Don't bother come back without Idris Elba,' said Melody. 'Make sure you wrap him up nice, sprinkle some pepper and jerk sauce on him, and bring him come to me.'

'He's married,' I said.

'Do me look like me care?' laughed Melody.

'You're too bad,' said Sienna. 'But while you're at it, can you bring me back the King's crown, Meghan Markle's wardrobe and some English tea.'

'English tea?' I repeated. 'You never drink English tea in all your life, Sienna Hudson. And Meghan live with Harry in America now.'

Long Goodbyes

'Me still want her wardrobe,' Sienna insisted. 'She must have left some clothes in the palaces and a warehouse full of name-brand shoes.'

We bantered until the cicadas started their nightly quarrels.

Mum picked me up at half-nine. She could've boiled enough water from our tears to make two English cups of tea.

'You all right, Kadeen?' Mum asked.

'Not really,' I replied.

'Me know you're going to miss your friends,' Mum said. 'But before you know it, you'll be back home again. Everyting will be OK.'

'Me really hope so.'

6

Flight to Greyland

For a leaving present, Mum bought me a red pair of Puma trainers to match my football boots. They didn't go with my black Puma tracksuit, but I wore them anyway. Mum fixed yellow, green and black beads in my braids. 'You might be leaving Jamaica, but you're carrying a small part of your island in your hair.'

Dad sneaked me three hundred American dollars to buy winter clothes.

'Don't tell your mother,' he warned. 'She's always telling me, me spoil you. Me don't want the grief.'

'But she already sent Aunt Mel some money for me,' I said.

'Aunt Mel don't need to know you have money.' Dad side-eyed me. 'Just keep it between ourselves. It's me contribution.'

'Me feel bad,' I admitted.

'You'll feel even worse when Aunt Mel pick out your clothes. You remember the trainers she buy for you from Brixton Market?'

I laughed out loud. 'She don't pop any style.'

'What you two talking about?' Mum called from the kitchen.

'Oh . . . nothing,' Dad replied. 'Just telling Kadeen to behave herself when she reach England.'

'Now, Hubert,' Mum went on. 'Don't drive too fast when you take us to the airport, you hear me? And your front right tyre bald like me grandfather head-top.'

'Me hear you.'

Mum had made me a packed lunch of plantain chips, an orange and a bun and cheese sandwich. I was already full of my favourite breakfast: roasted breadfruit, fried festival and dumpling, ackee and saltfish. I hunted it down with a mango, blackberry, banana and strawberry smoothie.

Dad joined me in the feast. He'd never admit it, but one thing he missed about Mum was her cooking. Edson loved it too, sometimes swiping a fried dumpling from my plate.

When he wasn't driving his work van, Dad steered a white Toyota Estate car. I caught a sadness in his eyes as he lifted my suitcases into the boot.

'You all right, Dad?'

'Yes, me all right. Look after yourself good, and don't eat

The Girl With the Red Boots

no meat if it pink inside. Oh, and don't talk to any strange boys. Remember, at that age they only want one ting.'

'Men want the one ting at any age,' cut in Mum.

I settled into the front seat. Mum sat behind me. She gave my shoulder a reassuring squeeze as Dad pulled away.

The road to Kingston simmered as it always did. Every other driver palmed their horn when we were caught up in traffic. The trucks were particularly intimidating. I tried to ignore it and read the messages on my phone. Melody and Sienna had sent a few.

> Kadeen, make sure your Aunt Mel buy you a coat thick like King Charles's coronation robe.

> Remember, if you ever forget, the sun is a round yellow ting in the sky.

> Love you bad, bad, bad, but me well happy me don't have to step in any goal for the time being.

> I'll keep a watch on Cass Buckley for you.

> Especially when he strips off and runs around the track.

> Make sure you bring back the English accent wid you.

> And Idris Elba.

Flight to Greyland

> And bring back some English crumpet – me always wonder what they taste like.

We arrived at Norman Manley International Airport two and a half hours before my departure time. I gave myself a moment before I climbed out of the car.

I read another message from Sienna.

> Cass Buckley is looking well fine today!
> Me just see him in him shorts, ready for sports.

Once again, I couldn't stem my tears.

Mum took out a tissue, wiped my face and kissed me on the forehead. She started to sing me Bob Marley's 'Three Little Birds', telling me it would all be OK.

I didn't feel any better.

The night drifted in over the airport. Lights pricked the steep hills overlooking Kingston harbour, and the taxis braked hard and pulled away too fast at the drop-off point.

Dad cussed one speeding driver as he wheeled my suitcase towards the departure building. I carried my ball in my left hand and pulled my red cabin case in the other.

When we arrived, he stroked my chin with his right index finger, smiled and said, 'Never forget, we all love you. Give me best to Aunt Mel, and don't boot your ball inside her yard.'

The Girl With the Red Boots

'Remember, Kadeen,' Mum said. 'Aunt Mel is going to enrol you into a local school. *Don't* chat back to the teachers and do your best work.'

'And join the school football team,' I added. 'If they have one.'

'*Don't* do anyting to bring yourself attention,' Mum warned. 'There are bad people out there. Keep your good self under a low profile. You understand?'

'Yes, me understand.'

Mum offered me one of her looks. She could only maintain it for two seconds as her eyes filled with tears. She caressed a stray hair from my face before she kissed me on the cheek. 'Be good!'

'Me always good.'

'Hmmmm.'

It suddenly licked me that this would be my first trip abroad on my lonesome. Mum, Dad and Edson had been always with me. 'Now, Kadeen,' Edson would say. 'You can't play keepy-uppy wid your ball on the plane. And keep your mout' quiet when you're munching your plantain chips. And use your wipes when you go to the bathroom. We don't want you picking up anyting.'

Who would be sitting next to me on my flight? It was usually Edson. Can I fill in the customs and immigration forms correctly? Will Aunt Mel be waiting for me at the airport?

My parents watched me join the bag-drop queue for British Airways. When I checked in my suitcase, they gave me a final wave.

Flight to Greyland

You're on your own now, Kadeen. Me going to miss me family and friends, but at least the mad-bad Tony Buttons can't trouble me.

I went through security without any worries. Every other shop sold rum or Bob Marley T-shirts. The number of fridge magnets on sale could have pulled in a cruise ship from Ocho Rios. Mum had instructed me to buy Captain Morgan's Private Stock for Aunt Mel. It was an expensive rum, but I guessed she needed something to keep her warm in the English winter. They didn't ask me for my ID.

I bought a football magazine for my flight and checked I had all my fave songs by Koffee, Protoje and Chronixx on my phone.

As my departure time approached, I felt increasingly nervous.

Is this really necessary? Maybe me can go back through security and go home. Tony Buttons don't know me. Me image was never published in a newspaper. Me name was never broadcast over radio. Him can't recognise me.

The idea escaped my mind as my departure time approached. It was an all-night flight, landing at Heathrow Airport just after 7 a.m. UK time.

Mum had booked me a window spot. I placed my small pillow between the top corner of my seat and the window, pulled my headphones over my head and tried to get as comfortable as possible.

As we accelerated on the runway, I thought of the home I just left and how happy I was to grow up in it. Edson never complained when he had to babysit me, and he always brought me with him when he was visiting friends or playing ball with them. *Now it'll be empty. Dad will be dropping Mum off to Aunt Doreen in May Pen, and he'll be heading back to Montego Bay to Monica and Simone. And I'm flying to the greyest country in the world to stay with the strictest aunt in the universe. All because of this devil pickney Tony Buttons.*

Damn him.

7

Aunt Mel

I managed to catch some sleep during the flight. The rice and chicken dinner wasn't too bad, but the scrambled egg breakfast was soggy. I probably overdosed on Diet Coke. Mum would have never allowed me to drink so much.

Kadeen! By the time you reach fifteen you will have no teeth in your head! And when you eat, all people will hear is the smacking of your gums. Learn to drink water.

I was glad to stretch my legs as I reached for my cabin case and my football. Despite wearing two T-shirts under my tracksuit top, I felt the chill as soon as I left the plane.

Gosh, I'm in England. Alone. I have bad-talked Aunt Mel, but me pray she's there to meet me.

Going through security and customs took me just over forty minutes. I had to wait a further twenty minutes for my red suitcase to appear on the carousel.

The Girl With the Red Boots

I immediately recognised Aunt Mel. She was wearing her knee-length black coat, a blue scarf that was long enough to wrap around Buckingham Palace, black leggings and black leather ankle boots. She had put on a couple of doses of weight since the last time I saw her. Her square glasses were a bit too small for her and her brown handbag looked no bigger than a purse. She wore an old-school gold watch on her left wrist. She was eight years older than my mum, but some might guess it was eighteen.

She gave me a one-armed hug.

Her straightened hair felt wiry, and I spotted tiny flecks of grey near her temples. I remembered she was fifty-one this year.

'How was your flight, Kadeen? You had someting to eat?'

'The flight not too bad,' I replied. 'It was a liccle bumpy about two hours into it, but it settle down from there. Me ate a liccle someting on the plane.'

'Good, good! Why you bring your football wid you? England cold right now, you don't want to catch your death playing in the chill.'

'Me's a football player, Aunt Mel,' I replied. 'Me friends tell me I'm good.'

'You always believe anyting your friends say?' challenged Aunt Mel. 'You don't come to play football. Your mother tell me to keep you safe, make sure you keep up to your schoolwork and to keep a low profile.'

How many weeks of this will me have to put up wid? Me hope they catch bad-breed, devil pickney Tony Buttons today.

Aunt Mel

Aunt Mel led me to the Underground station. We caught a tube to Green Park before we changed for the Victoria line.

So many people travelling on the Underground. Me hope the train don't stop in the middle of the tunnel and the roof don't fall in on we.

We arrived in Brixton about ten minutes later. I rubbed my hands warm when we stepped out into the open air. It was still strange watching smoky-white breath puff out of everybody's mouths.

There were as many people buzzing around Brixton Tube station as downtown Kingston. They wore puffy jackets, wrap-around scarves, cockroach-crushing boots and all kinds of hats. Everyone was going about their business so much quicker.

'You're cold, Kadeen? Don't worry. I'll buy you a jacket in the market tomorrow morning.'

'In the market?' I repeated.

'You don't want to waste good money on name-brand this and name-brand that. There's nothing wrong wid a nice warm jacket from the market.'

I sighed, but not too loud.

Aunt Mel lived on Josephine Avenue, just off Brixton Hill. The terraced houses were tall, and the trees swayed in the cold breeze. It was weird seeing naked branches. Brockwell Park was nearby, but I guessed I wouldn't be spending too much time there.

Like Mum, Aunt Mel was a quick walker. We arrived at her ground-floor flat in just over ten minutes.

She had two bedrooms, a cramped kitchen smelling of herbs and spices, and a square front room where the three-piece suite struggled to fit. There was a flat-screen TV fixed to the wall, and I hoped Aunt Mel would allow me to watch what I wanted instead of 24/7 Sky News and police dramas.

Framed photographs of my family, including Mum, Gran and Granddad, hung from the walls. Books including Zadie Smith's *White Teeth*, Andrea Levy's *Small Island* and Yvonne Bailey-Smith's *The Day I Fell Off My Island* filled a small bookshelf. On a shelf, a wooden carving of a doctor bird, a toy Jamaican basketball player, a glass tankard displaying a map of Jamaica and a small drum reminded Aunt Mel of her home island.

Out back, Aunt Mel didn't do too much with her small garden. What I could see of it was overgrown.

Hardly any room to play keepy-uppy there.

'You want to take your rest now, or do you want me to fry you a liccle someting? It's still breakfast time.'

'I'll have someting to eat, please,' I replied. 'Me will sleep after that. Thank you.'

Aunt Mel cooked me scrambled eggs and bacon and served it with two slices of buttered hard-dough bread. It tasted much better than what I picked at on the plane.

I was disappointed when I discovered there was no TV in my room.

How am I going to watch Premier League football or any other sports? It's bad enough not having access to Netflix.

Instead, there was a desk in the corner where a laptop

Aunt Mel

rested, and more books inside a bedside cabinet. A polished brown wooden cross kept watch over the bed. Beige-coloured paint blessed the walls.

I unpacked my suitcase and remembered to give Aunt Mel her bottle of rum.

'Thank you, thank you so much,' she said. 'Last time your mother forget, but she remember. Me will call her later.'

'Me going to try and catch a liccle sleep,' I said.

I put my phone on charge, closed the blinds and slipped into bed.

The sheets are cold!

It didn't take me too long to doze off.

Like Superman, I was zooming back to Jamaica, through skinny clouds and then endless blue sky, passing the occasional doctor bird. I wore a black, gold and green cape and black boots. I felt a hot sun blazing on my back. Expensive yachts sailed the calm seas beneath me. I looked down and could see Kingston harbour. Long cargo ships offloaded their goods. Tall cranes whirred here and there. Planes took off from the nearby airport every other minute.

I flew towards Old Harbour and dived down to the square. People huddled around the clocktower. They all wore black. Sorrow marked their faces. A white pick-up truck screeched and swerved away. Dust flew up in its wake. Tony Buttons cackled a horrible cackle.

'*Murder!*' someone cried out.

The crowd backed away and dispersed. One body

remained. Lying on the ground in the middle of the square was Edson. He seemed to be sleeping. His left cheek kissed the concrete. Blood spilled from his right ear. Half of his nose was missing, like a bird with a sharp beak had pecked away at it. Suddenly, his eyes opened.

'Murderer! Blood upon your shoulder!'

'Aaaaaarrrggghhh!'

I sat upright in bed. I had been dreaming. I wiped sweat from my face and reached to switch on the lamp on the bedside cabinet.

Aunt Mel burst into my room like she was ready to do battle with the Antichrist.

'What happen to you, child?' she asked. 'You scream like the devil come to take you.'

I couldn't rid the image of Edson's dead body from my mind. Feeling the draught from the window, I crossed my arms, dropped my head and cried.

Aunt Mel sat down beside me and wrapped an arm around my shoulders. Her cheeks curved into a reassuring smile. 'Is it Edson?' she asked.

I nodded.

'He's not gone.' She smiled. 'He's looking over you. Not in body, but in spirit. And he'll always be there. He's in a good place where the angels will look after him. And he will make them laugh wid his jokes. They will prepare a seat for him at their table. He'll be eating the sweet bread of tomorrow and sipping the wine of eternity. Oh, yes. Hallelujah. Don't worry about that.'

Aunt Mel

'You truly believe that, Aunt Mel?'

'Of course.' She nodded. 'You must have suffered a nightmare.'

'Yes. Me see him. Up close. Edson look like him was sleeping. He didn't seem dead. Then . . . then his eyes opened . . .'

'As me was saying, a bad dream you suffer, but Edson living a good dream where everyting is nice. He's in a place where pain and trauma is no more. Think of it that way.'

'Me will try.'

'Do you want me to lie down wid you for a liccle while?'

I thought about it.

'No, thank you for offering, but me will be all right.'

'You sure?'

'Me sure,' I replied.

8

Brixton

The next morning, Aunt Mel woke me just before 10 a.m. I enjoyed a breakfast of fried eggs, baked beans and mushrooms on toast before we left to go to the market. Aunt Mel informed me what she was about to buy.

'The fish in the arcade is cheaper than the fish store on the street,' she said. 'Me feel like some fresh mackerel. You like mackerel, Kadeen?'

'Yes, please.' I nodded.

I thought of Shelly's Place by Old Harbour Bay, and the fishermen who went out to sea in their small boats.

Sienna will be celebrating her birthday there in a few days. But I'm in Greyland.

Before Aunt Mel purchased her mackerel and other groceries, she stopped by a market stall and bought me a black puffy jacket. Her haggling won her a three-pound discount. Aunt Mel grinned a triumphant grin. As the vendor shook his head, I tried it on. When I pulled the hood over my head, it drowned me. I can't lie, it was snug and warm, but it didn't exactly show off my figure. I had never worn anything this big and heavy in my life.

'Perfect!' said Aunt Mel. 'Now you can't complain about the cold. Pull the hood over your head.'

'It's like wearing a duvet on street,' I protested.

'Stop complain. It'll keep your backside warm. This is England. When the cold wind blows, it rips off the flesh and nibbles your bones.'

'You're not wrong there.'

'Come, Kadeen, me want to show you the school.'

Aunt Mel quick-marched me to Coldharbour Lane. I felt the chill in my toes as we passed the Brixton House theatre (Sienna would have loved checking that place out) and made a right into Somerleyton Road.

We passed a mural of a dead rapper called Ty. I stopped to take a pic on my phone and made a mental note to Google him later. 'Come, Kadeen. Don't lag behind or wander off! Brixton can be a dangerous place.'

I watched the cold-bitten faces and grim expressions around me and wondered how Aunt Mel had survived in this frozen land for more than fifteen years.

We turned left at the top of the road. Evelyn Grace Academy was situated on the right-hand side of Loughborough Park. Near the entrance, they had a short running track with four lanes. Never seen that facility in a Jamaican school. Cass

The Girl With the Red Boots

Buckley and his friends would love that. I spotted several table tennis tables in the playground, but all seemed quiet. I wondered if they had any girls' football teams.

'I have already spoken to the headteacher,' Aunt Mel said. 'He's a good friend of mine. He understands your situation and wants to help. Nobody else in the school knows your business. He agrees that your education shouldn't have to suffer. It's a good school, and if you spend two days or two months there, you'll do well. I have already ordered your uniform.'

'Uniform?' I repeated.

'Yes, you'll be required to wear black trousers, a blazer and tie.'

'When do me pick it up?'

'It will be mailed to me,' Aunt Mel replied. 'It should come in the next few days. Your mother sent me your size.'

Before we went home, Aunt Mel led me to Windrush Square. It was opposite the town hall, next door to the library. The grass felt crunchy beneath my feet. The chill didn't deter a pair of drinkers who had wet noses and cracked lips.

Aunt Mel explained to me that following the Second World War, many people arrived from the Caribbean to settle in the UK and help the *'motherland'* rebuild.

'Most of the Jamaicans came to Brixton,' she said. 'And many of the small-islanders went to Ladbroke Grove.'

'Mum did tell me a liccle someting about Great-Aunt Edna.'

Brixton

'Me Aunt Edna come here wid a British passport,' Aunt Mel explained. 'Yes, she was so proud to own it. She was a nurse. She always wanted to go back to Jamaica to live out her days, but she never did. She died too early. That won't happen to me. Oh, no, sah!'

'Me pray for you it don't,' I replied.

Aunt Mel's phone sang a Bob Marley song. 'No Woman, No Cry'. She answered it and looked at me.

'It's your mum, but the connection bad,' she said. 'Come, Kadeen, let's walk home and call her back when we reach.'

Maybe the police catch this wolf-heart, Tony Buttons. They shouldn't bother wid a trial for him. Just fling him into Kingston harbour with concrete tied to him foot and let the harbour-sharks taste bad-breed flesh.

I was glad to feel the warmth of Aunt Mel's central heating. We made for the kitchen, where Aunt Mel switched on the kettle.

'Tea?' she offered.

Hot drinks weren't my thing, but it would help warm me up. I hadn't taken off my new jacket.

'Yes, thanks.'

Three sips later, Aunt Mel called Mum. She put her phone on speaker.

'Can you hear me OK?' Aunt Mel asked.

'Yes,' Mum replied. 'Me hear you good. Everyting all right?'

'Yes, everyting good. Me take Kadeen to Brixton Market this morning and buy her a jacket. She well happy wid it.'

I side-eyed Aunt Mel.

'Everyting good your side?' Aunt Mel asked.

'Not really,' Mum replied. I moved a little closer to the phone. 'Last night me hear some disturbing news from the police. They come to me yard after nine.'

Aunt Mel glanced at me before taking another sip from her tea. Steam rose from it. I wrapped my hands around my mug. I moved a little closer to the phone.

'What disturbing news?' Aunt Mel wanted to know.

'Is Kadeen there?'

'Yes, me here, Mum.'

'Good, becah this concerns you.'

'What concerns me, Mum?'

'Stop take long journey around the bull pen and tell we what ah gwaan,' Aunt Mel insisted.

There was a long moment of silence.

'It's Tony Buttons,' Mum finally revealed. 'CCTV spotted him at Kingston Airport. The police said he boarded a Jet Blue flight to Miami. They believe he's travelling on a false passport.'

A cold chill twisted around my ribs and curled around my spine.

'How can a somebody who is one of Jamaica's most wanted just stroll around Kingston Airport and jump on a flight to Miami?' Aunt Mel asked. 'What the police doing? Them have any sense? Did the police at the airport even know they're meant to be looking for this terrorist Tony Buttons? Do they have eyes in their heads?'

Brixton

'Mel, me don't know what dem doing!' Mum replied. 'Officer Crystal Myers couldn't even look me in the eye. Shame, she feel shame.'

'So,' I cut in. 'He . . . he could be anywhere. Miami Airport big. You can fly anywhere. Including England.'

'That is true.' Aunt Mel nodded. 'But Jamaican security must have informed the American officials so they can arrest him when him walk off the flight.'

'The flight already landed before the Americans received the information,' Mum said. 'He went through customs wid a false passport. They don't know where him is.'

Aunt Mel and I shared another concerned look.

'You . . .' I began. 'You think he might come to England?'

'Don't upset yourself,' replied Aunt Mel. 'This Tony Buttons can't have too many false passports. They take your fingerprints and a photo of you before they let you in the country.'

'Him get through,' I said. 'Maybe he's coming for me?'

'Stop that kinda talk,' said Mum. 'There could be a million reasons why him fly to Miami. Remember, he don't even know your name or what you look like.'

'Me hope you're not wrong,' I replied.

'Let me change the subject,' said Mum. 'How is England?'

'The cold is showing its teeth,' I said. 'It's grey like me remember it. And it's not even snowing yet. Aunt Mel buy me a jacket to keep out the frost.'

'Did you thank her?'

I turned to Aunt Mel. 'Thank you.'

'You're starting school next week,' Mum reminded me. 'Try not to worry yourself about the Tony Buttons ting and concentrate on your schoolwork.'

'Me will try.'

'And help out Aunt Mel around the house.'

'Yes, me will.'

I sat back. Aunt Mel and Mum caught up on family gossip, rumours and the low value of the Jamaican dollar.

I went to my room and fretted about Tony Buttons. I never saw how tall he was inside the pick-up truck, but my nightmares were telling me he was at least seven foot six. He also owned a fist that was bigger than my face. I imagined his weapon of choice was a rocket launcher that had my name on it.

Sleep must have caught up with me because Aunt Mel shook me awake. She had cooked a roasted mackerel dinner in peppers and onions and served it with boiled potatoes, spinach and carrots. I hunted it down with orange juice.

'It's Friday tomorrow, Kadeen,' she said. 'I'm going into work in the morning but coming home at lunchtime. Just rest yourself and take it easy; the jet lag must be still in your system. Remember, don't wander off to places you don't know. Keep yourself to yourself. *Don't* speak to strangers.'

9

Brockwell Park

The next morning before Aunt Mel went to work, she asked me to season four chicken thighs and place them in the fridge, ready to cook. As soon as she left, I did what I was asked, and I also peeled carrots and chopped a cabbage. I wanted to earn some Brockwell Park points.

It was just after nine when my football gave me some side-eye.

Studs and kneecaps! Me don't bring me football all the way from Jamaica just to look at it. What would Edson do?

I went to my room, picked up my red football boots from my suitcase and pulled on an old tracksuit.

I made my way to the park, jogging most of the way to keep warm.

This is not wandering off. I know my way to and from the park.

The Girl With the Red Boots

Although the grass in parts was long and the ground muddy, I imagined I was playing in Wembley Stadium, Camp Nou in Barcelona or Old Trafford, Manchester. I practised my step overs and Cruyff turns. I led with my left foot and then on to my right.

Try to use your left foot, I remembered Edson training me. *A two-footed player is a treasure.*

I slipped over a couple of times, staining my tracksuit. I tried keepy-uppy with my head, reaching fourteen nods. I slid into a puddle and tasted mud.

Me hope me can remember how to use the washing machine. Aunt Mel going to cuss me behind for playing football in the park. Me better wash it before she reach home.

Someone giggled.

I looked over my shoulder.

Sitting on a park bench was this blonde girl. She was wearing a grimy yellow puffy jacket and black jeans. Freckles dotted her nose. Her false eyelashes could've imitated a Harry Potter spider. Bruised trainers wrapped her feet. She looked about my age.

'Excuse me,' I said. 'You laughing at me?'

'I didn't see anyone else making friends with the mud.' She grinned. 'You're good though. A proper baller.'

'Yes, so me friends tell me,' I replied.

'Are you from Jamaica?' she asked. 'You talk like Miss Delaney, the Jamaican lady who lives two floors up from us.'

'Yes, me born and grow in Jamaica. A place call Old

Harbour. Where they sell the best fish and bammy on the island.'

'You here on holiday?'

'Sort of,' I replied.

'Kinda weird to come to the UK in February for a holiday,' she said. 'Most people round here holiday at Butlin's in Bognor or nip down to Brighton on a sunny day.'

'As me said, it's a sort of holiday. Me can't really explain.'

'I see you're good when you have no defenders to dribble around,' she chuckled. 'You wanna try me?'

I thought about it.

'It's a bit muddy,' I said. 'And you're not wearing any boots. Me don't want you to stain and wet up yourself.'

'What's a bit of grime?' she replied.

'OK,' I agreed. 'By the way, what's your name?'

'Louella,' she replied. 'Louella Elms.'

'Kadeen Best,' I said.

Louella proved a difficult defender to pass. Her tackles were hard and crunchy. If I tried to go around her, she would ram her shoulder into me. She should've been an American footballer.

'That's a foul!' I protested.

'I don't see no referee,' she laughed. 'Football's a physical game. Get used to it.'

I tried to nutmeg her, but she closed her legs in time.

'Saw that coming,' she said. 'You got any other skills?'

I came at her again. This time I tried three step overs,

The Girl With the Red Boots

dropped my left shoulder, feinted to my left and moved to my right. Finally, I passed her.

'And it's one nil to Jamaica in the World Cup final!'

Louella placed her hands on her hips and smiled. 'You just beat me once! In Jamaica, do you play for a team?'

'No,' I replied. 'My school focuses on track, cricket and basketball.'

'A shame; you would make a good winger. You're tricky and speedy.'

'You really think so?'

'Yes,' she said. 'You got around me, didn't you?'

I picked up the ball and we stepped to the bench.

'How long is your sort of holiday?' Louella asked.

I shrugged. 'Not sure. It could be a week, a month or longer.'

Louella looked confused. 'Wish I could go on a holiday for a year in Jamaica. All those nice beaches. Hot sun. Reggae music and jerk chicken patties. But I've never sat my ass down in a plane.'

'You're telling me jokes, right,' I replied.

Louella shook her head. I noticed a dose of sadness in her eyes. 'I'm serious – never heard a stewardess say, "And now please secure your safety belts ready for take-off."'

I decided to change the subject. 'Shouldn't . . . shouldn't you be in school?'

'Yeah, I should be,' Louella replied. 'But I got up today and I thought, screw it.'

'You don't like school?' I wondered.

'Sometimes. It's just some girls there love to take the piss. If you don't wear name-brand clothes, have your nails done every day and wear make-up like a prom queen, they think there's something wrong with you.'

'Shallow,' I said.

'Yeah.' Louella nodded. 'Shallow like an ant's spit.'

'Do you play for any team?' I asked.

'Yeah.' Louella nodded. 'The SW2s.'

'The SW2s?' I repeated.

'Yeah, most of us live in the postcode SW2. A few live in SW9, so we make them pay bigger subs.'

'That's harsh,' I said.

'Just joking.'

'What competitions do you play in?'

'We're in the South London Women's League,' Louella replied. 'I play right back. We're doing good this year, second in the league.'

'That's brilliant,' I said.

'Do you wanna have a trial with us? We could do with a few extra players. We haven't got much back-up for injuries. Our goalkeeper had period pains last week and I had to go in goal. We lost three-one. It wasn't pretty. Second game we lost this season.'

I thought about it.

Louella isn't a stranger. Me made good friends wid her. She's hardly going to know Tony Buttons. Aunt Mel might still be against it though. She's mega-cautious. But do me just go to this new school, come home, get up in the morning, go back to the school and do nothing else?

'Me . . . me not too sure. Me have to talk to me aunt first. You understand?'

'It'll be a shame to waste your step overs just on me.'

I laughed out loud then looked at the mud that had collected on my tracksuit bottoms. 'Me better fast-forward home and wash me clothes,' I said.

'Where do you live?' Louella asked.

'Josephine Avenue,' I replied. 'And you?'

'Tulse Hill estate, just opposite the park. Fifth floor. Osgood House.'

Louella took out a biro from her jacket pocket. 'What's your phone number,' she asked.

I gave her my digits and she wrote it down on her right palm.

'I'll ding you,' she promised. 'We train on Wednesdays.'

'Where?'

'Battersea Park. They have floodlit artificial pitches.'

'Where's that?'

'On the other side of Clapham Junction.'

I shook my head. 'Where's Clapham Junction?'

'Don't worry,' said Louella. 'I get picked up. You can catch a ride with me if your aunt allows it.'

'OK, see you later.'

'Yep, laters.'

I made my way out of the park.

Brockwell Park

When I arrived home, I pulled off my tracksuit, threw it in the washing machine and pushed all the buttons.

Nothing happened.

Socks and shin pads!

I tried to work it out.

Damn! I didn't switch the plug on.

I managed to get it working.

Relief!

As I waited for the machine to complete its cycle, I called Sienna on WhatsApp.

'Kadeen, it's not even six o'clock yet,' Sienna said. 'Don't you have any mercy for the sleepers of this world?'

'Me wanted to catch you before you left for school,' I replied.

'You wanted to show off and tell me about how you looked up at Big Ben and twerked down the corridors of Buckingham Palace.'

'Me don't do any sightseeing yet,' I said. 'It's too damn cold for that. Buckingham Palace and the Tower of London can wait. When me take off me trainers yesterday, me had to count me toes to check if dem all there. Me still can't feel dem.'

'Better you're in the English cold rather than Jamaica,' Sienna said.

'Why you say that?' I asked.

'You don't see the front page of *The Star* newspaper?' Sienna wondered.

The Girl With the Red Boots

'Sienna! Me here in England. How me going to sight the front page of *The Star*?'

There was a five-second pause.

'Sienna? You still there?'

'Yes, me here. Me just screenshot the front page and me sending it to you.'

'What's it all about?'

'Tony Buttons,' Sienna revealed. 'Everybody talking about it at school. Even the teachers and probably the lizards in the gulley.'

'Talking about what?'

'About how him turn up at Kingston Airport in a white baseball cap and no police arrest him.'

'A white baseball cap?' I repeated. 'Mum never tell me that.'

'In the paper, they listed all his alleged crimes,' Sienna added. 'His mum must be ashamed of him. And him granny, teachers and him church minister too!'

'What crimes?'

'You sure you want to know? It's a list of pure shame. When me read it, me blood turned a different shade of dread.'

'Yes, me want to know,' I insisted.

'He's suspected of four murders, two robberies, whole heap of kidnapping, untold serious assaults and more unspeakable things.'

'Oh my gosh,' I said.

I put my hand over my mouth.

'Me don't finish yet,' cut in Sienna. 'He's also alleged to have wounded a police officer with gunshot, importing drugs and firearms, and some kinda money fraud. When it come to crime, Tony Buttons well versatile.'

I sucked in a long breath. 'Four murders?'

'Yes, two in Jamaica and two in Belize.'

'Him badder than bad,' I said.

'As he's left Jamaica,' Sienna replied, 'you might as well come back to Old Harbour.'

'Me don't know, Sienna.'

'It make sense.' Sienna raised her voice. 'Bad-breed Tony Buttons outta the country. Let him do him badness in Belize, Miami or wherever. And in the US, the police shoot first and ask questions later. That's a good policy when it come to Satan pickney like Tony Buttons.'

'Me hope somebody arrest him quick-time.'

'Me too,' Sienna agreed.

'Me miss you,' I admitted.

'Me miss you too,' she said.

'How is Melody?' I asked.

'Melody! Melody take a liking to Wilson McKenzie. Can you believe it? We sight him broad chest and long forehead in Juici Pattie yesterday. Him come over to wish me a happy birthday and Melody flutter she eye like a butterfly on drugs.'

'But your birthday's tomorrow?' I pointed out.

'Yes, me know that. Hear the tale. Melody want Wilson to come to me birthday treat at Shelly's Place.'

'Me thought it was for close family and friends,' I queried. 'Not for guys that tickle Melody's like button.'

'But how do me tell her that? Melody want a party on the beach after everybody eat.'

I heard another voice. Sienna's mum. 'Sienna! It's six o'clock. Stop chat your foolishness on the phone and get ready for school!'

'Me will catch up wid you later,' Sienna promised. 'Don't steal the Crown Jewels.'

'And you don't allow Melody to invite the whole of Old Harbour to your birthday treat. Happy birthday!'

'You buy me anyting yet?'

'Wait till me come home.'

'Sienna!' I heard in the background.

Sienna killed the call.

10

Aunt Mel's Date

The spin cycle of the washing machine finished moments before Aunt Mel arrived home. I quickly folded my tracksuit and placed it in a chest of drawers in my room. It was still a bit damp. Aunt Mel carried in bags of shopping.

'You had a good morning?' she asked. 'You been resting yourself?'

'Er, yes, you know. The jet lag still in me legs.'

'After another good night's sleep, you'll be all right.'

'Yes, me hope so.'

Aunt Mel placed three lamb shanks in the fridge. She had also bought parsnips, baby potatoes and more carrots.

'Me have a guest coming to dinner tomorrow,' she announced.

'Oh? A friend?'

'Yes . . . a friend. Me know him from work.'

The Girl With the Red Boots

'He works at the town hall?'

'Yes, finance. I work in the housing department.'

'So . . . this friend. He's your boyfriend?'

My grin bust out of my cheeks.

Aunt Mel turned away from me as she dropped the parsnips on to the kitchen counter.

'We just . . . keep each other company . . . sometimes, you know. Lunch, tea break, that kinda ting. Now and again we catch a liccle drink after work. He just come back from burying his mother in Barbados.'

'Sorry to hear,' I said.

'He's had a rough time. So me want to cook him someting nice, you know.'

I couldn't kill my smile. 'Yes, me know.'

I helped Aunt Mel season the lamb before we placed it in a sealed bowl and left it in the fridge.

'You never tink about getting married, Aunt Mel? All me other aunts and uncles, except mad Uncle Phillip, are married.'

'Uncle Phillip? Him married to his chickens, his goats, his music and him Dragon Stout. He'll never divorce them for anybody.'

Aunt Mel paused from placing a loaf of bread into the bread bin. She looked out the window before she turned round to face me.

Boots and corner flags! Was it appropriate to ask her about marriage? Mum's always telling me to know my size and age and stop ask big people big questions.

Aunt Mel's Date

Aunt Mel dropped into a chair at the small kitchen table. 'Yes,' she said finally. 'Since me come here me been hoping that maybe . . . one day, I might meet someone.'

'No luck?'

'Me been close two or three times,' she revealed. 'But when it come to it, they didn't want to commit, not even to live together, you know.'

'Me sorry to hear,' I said.

'Me soon fifty-one and black hair dye is now me good, good friend,' Aunt Mel admitted. 'Me never really wanted children. That was the problem in two relationships . . .'

Awkward silence.

'Me . . .' I began. 'Me hope tomorrow goes well for you.'

'Thank you.'

The following afternoon I boiled the vegetables with a pinch of thyme and mint as Aunt Mel roasted the lamb shanks in foil. The smell was delicious. Alvin, her date, arrived with a bottle of Prosecco at 7 p.m. He looked younger than Aunt Mel, maybe late thirties or early forties. Like most black men these days, he had shaved his head and grew a beard. He was dressed in immaculate white trainers, jeans and a denim jacket. Aunt Mel made the introductions.

'And you never tell me how pretty your niece is,' he said in a Bajan accent as he gave me a one-armed hug.

'Nice to meet you,' I managed. 'You . . . you need some time to catch up so me going to me room.'

The Girl With the Red Boots

I carried my tray of dinner with me, sat in front of the laptop and switched it on.

An hour or so later I was enjoying YouTube reels of my favourite football players, Khadija Shaw, Alexia Putellas, Oshoala, Lauren James and Sam Kerr, when I heard raised voices from the kitchen.

I took off my headphones and concentrated my ears.

'Can't we see how things go,' Alvin shouted. 'All this pressure. I don't need it.'

'We've known each other for well over three years,' Aunt Mel replied. 'Me just want to know where we're going. What's wrong wid asking that?'

'I just lost my mother,' Alvin said.

'And I've just lost my nephew!'

What do I do? Shall I stay in my room and wait till it's all over, pretend me never hear anyting? Yes, just stay here so. Don't bust into big people's business. It'll only make tings awkward.

I continued to listen.

'Alvin, life goes on,' Aunt Mel said. 'Me nearly touching fifty-one. Me need to know if we have a future together. Me don't have time to waste.'

There was a long pause. Suddenly a chair screeched. Plates, knives and forks clattered in the sink. Someone turned on a tap.

'I'm ... I'm sorry, Mel. You know I was married once. The divorce was ... Well, you know what that did to me. I don't really want to get married again.'

Aunt Mel's Date

'Is that it?' Aunt Mel asked. 'This is what all the dates, lunches, dinners have led to? That you can't commit to me? And it's only now you're telling me?'

'I . . . I better leave.'

A few moments of silence before I heard the front door open and close.

What do me do now? Put me headphones back on and act like me never hear anyting? Or do me try and comfort Aunt Mel? She might want a liccle time on her own. Then again . . .

I switched my laptop off, inhaled a long breath and made my way to the kitchen.

Aunt Mel slouched at the table. A half-full glass of Prosecco was held loosely in her right hand. I thought at any moment she might spill it. In her other hand, she gripped the toy basketball player – I could just about see its head. She looked pretty in her green, yellow and black flower dress and her black headwrap. She had kicked off her black shoes. One was on the other side of the kitchen.

'Sit down,' she ordered.

I did what I was told.

'You ever drink Prosecco, Kadeen?'

I shook my head. 'Me never touch alcohol. When me was eight years old, Uncle Phillip give me a taste of Dragon Stout when Great-Grandma Ruby pass. That was enough for me. And you can't touch alcohol if you want to play professional football.'

'You're a good girl. Me sure your mother raise you well.'

'Are you all right, Aunt Mel?'

The Girl With the Red Boots

Aunt Mel took a generous sip from her glass. A dribble leaked from her lips. She locked her gaze on to me. 'No, Kadeen, me haven't been all right for a while.'

'Alvin?'

'Yes, Alvin. Me thought there was a future together, you know. It's not pushing it if me ask where the relationship is going after three years, is it?'

'Me . . . me don't know,' I replied.

'It's the same story,' added Aunt Mel, now studying her empty glass. 'There was Noel and Trevor. Now Alvin. None of them wanted to commit to me. None of them can match up to . . .'

She stopped talking and studied the model basketballer. It wore Jamaican colours. I wondered who gave her that gift.

'Do me look old to you, Kadeen?'

'Er, no, not at all. You still look good. Pretty.'

'Me keep myself in trim,' Aunt Mel said. 'Me work out and go to war wid my body every other day. Me not the prettiest girl in the world but me sure not the ugliest.'

I shook my head. Aunt Mel's head dropped towards the table.

'No, no way,' I managed. 'Dem don't deserve you.'

Aunt Mel glared at me like she wasn't convinced. She refilled her glass and took a sip before speaking again. 'You have a sweetheart back home in Old Harbour, Kadeen? A first love?'

I couldn't help but think of Cass Buckley.

Aunt Mel's Date

'No, not really,' I replied. 'Me don't think Mum would allow me to have a boyfriend.'

'What do you mean not really?'

'There's this guy at school who clicks me like button,' I admitted. 'But him older than me. Sixteen. Me don't even know if him ever notice me.'

'What's his name?' Aunt Mel wanted to know.

'Cass,' I replied. 'Cass Buckley.'

'When you're a liccle older, and if this Mr Cass Buckley is available, don't wait till your thirties or forties to make a play for him.'

'Me . . . me not sure if me will ever get the chance.'

'If the opportunity presents itself –' Aunt Mel leaned towards me – 'remember my advice. The truth is, Kadeen, that if you wait too long, your options run out. When you get to my age, the dating pool is full up of men who are divorced, don't want to commit, and the dangerous ones you must steer clear from. Hear me good. Me have experience of all three.'

Aunt Mel climbed out of her chair, carefully replaced the toy basketballer on the shelf and went to the fridge. She grabbed a tub of chocolate ice cream from the freezer. She collected two bowls from a cupboard and filled them with cold, dark pleasure. She picked out a teaspoon from a drawer.

'I'm taking this to me bed,' Aunt Mel said. 'Me usually try to stay away from chocolate, but hey, what the blasted hell?'

'Good . . . goodnight, Aunt Mel.'

'Goodnight, Kadeen.'

Aunt Mel back-heeled her bedroom door shut. I picked up a dessert spoon from the draining board and dug into my treat. It was soft and creamy and niced up my taste buds. I couldn't rid my mind of Cass Buckley and wondered if we'd ever date.

Probably not. Him probably have a girlfriend already.

I served myself another mouthful.

Before I went to my bed, I washed up the things in the sink and placed the Prosecco in the fridge. Mum would've been proud.

11

Dangerous Rumours

I woke up at 7.30 the next morning.

Sunday.

The flat was quiet as I went to pour myself a glass of water in the kitchen. I heard Aunt Mel snoring from her bedroom. Her door was open. Her black, green and yellow dress was in a crumpled heap beside her bed.

I went back to my room and decided to call Sienna. I knew it was the middle of the night in Jamaica, but I guessed she might be still up following her birthday night.

'Sienna . . . Sienna? Can you hear me?'

'Me hear you good, Kadeen.'

Her voice sounded sleepy.

'Why are you calling me so late? Lord have extra mercy! It's half past two in the morning! You never want me to sleep again?'

'Me wanted to know how your birthday went,' I said. 'You can't tell me that? Me's your best friend. Remember, me here so in the land of grey.'

'It was dramatic,' Sienna said. 'It was just me family and Melody at Shelly's Place, but liccle after seven, Wilson McKenzie and other friends from school come down. Somebody bring some music and a Bluetooth speaker. We were bubbling on the beach till midnight. Nuff dancing and nuff jokes.'

'Your parents allowed that?' I asked.

'They left about nine. They just tell me not to drink any alcohol and be back inside my yard by midnight.'

'We should call you Cinderella,' I giggled.

'Oh, and Wilson and Melody kiss up each other like dem star in a rom-com.'

'Seriously? No jokes?'

'Yes, me double serious! And it wasn't a joke ting. Everybody in Old Harbour see it. It's all over Instagram. Their picture might be on the front page of *The Star* tomorrow. Dem kiss for so long me was wondering if dem needed a special breathing mask to reboot dem chest. Me sure both of dem lips take ah bruise.'

'And me miss that big drama. Wow! Wilson and Melody. Could you ever believe it?'

'Melody went home wid a smile broader than a fat pumpkin! It will take a punch from Black Panther to wipe off Wilson's mighty grin.'

'So it sound like everybody had a good time?'

'Yes, me wish you was there, Kadeen,' Sienna said. 'Then it would've been perfect.'

I couldn't reply to that.

Damn bad-breed Tony Buttons!

'Kadeen? Kadeen? You still there?'

'Yes, me still here. Just swallowing a dose of sadness. Me miss Jamaica . . . me miss Old Harbour.'

'Oh, me forget to tell you,' Sienna said.

'Forget to tell me what?'

'Cass Buckley,' Sienna replied. 'Him come down to the Bay about half-ten to pick up him cousin, Nadine. Me never even know they were related.'

'Cass Buckley!' I repeated. 'Did he stay long?'

'About half an hour. Him buy a smoothie and sit down watching everybody dance. Before he left, he wished me a happy birthday and him ask for you. Can you believe that?'

'Lie you tell,' I yelled.

'No lie!' Sienna insisted. 'May Lord Jesus nail me to the cross and box me face if me tell a lie. Him say to me, "Where is your best friend, Kadeen? You two are always together."'

'Did he say anyting else?' I asked.

'Just that he heard about Edson and him send his condolences to you and your family.'

'So him know who me is?'

'For real.'

'When him ask where me there, how did him face look?'

'What do you mean how did him face look?'

'Did him say it like he missed me?' I asked. 'Like him like me?'

'Me don't know,' Sienna replied. 'His expression was just normal-like. Just be glad him ask for you.'

'And he wasn't wid a girl?'

'You don't listen to me, Kadeen? Him come alone to pick up his cousin. As far as me can see, he's single. You can blow out your relief.'

Sienna knew me too good. I did exactly what she said.

If Edson was still here me wonder how he would have got on with Cass if he was me boyfriend. Probably good. They both love sports.

'Oh, there's another ting you should know,' Sienna said.

'What's that?' I asked.

'Me was talking to Filbert Stanley, you know, that red-skin maaga boy in the year above we?'

'Yes, me know him. Him always eating barbecued chicken wings and large fries from KFC after school. And he never puts on weight. What did him say?'

'Him say that Tony Buttons' crew have people all over, including London.'

'London?' I repeated. 'Don't play wid me, Sienna! You sure?'

'Yes, that's what him say.'

'And how would him know?' I wanted confirmation.

'His dad's a policeman,' Sienna revealed. 'He works outta May Pen station.'

I tried to say something, but I couldn't get the words out. Small icicles filled my veins.

Me parents said London was safe for me. Maybe this is why Aunt Mel is so cautious about me going out and about.

'Kadeen . . . Kadeen?'

'Yes . . . me still here.'

'Don't bother fret about it too much,' said Sienna. 'There's a whole heap of rumour and talk. Me don't tink nobody know the real truth.'

'It could be true,' I said. 'Me dad used to tell me about the Spangler Posse and how dem reach New York, LA and London. Him tell me how ruthless they were and how dem terrorise and kill innocent people.'

'Me still tink you should come home,' Sienna said. 'Everywhere is a danger. Montego Bay, Trinidad, Cancún, everywhere. If you come home, at least you'll be wid people who love you.'

'Yes, me hear that.' I nodded. 'But Aunt Mel love me too.'

'Aunt Mel?' Sienna repeated. 'You tell me pure horror story about she?'

'She not too bad,' I said. 'Not bad at all. For years me think she had it easy. You know, living in England. She have a good job and ting. But me tink she a bit lonely. She want someone to share her life wid but she don't get no luck in that department.'

Before she let me go, Sienna gave me a full rundown of her party, including what new dances people performed, who twerked against who and how many guests splashed in the sea.

I could only shed a tear.

Four hours later, Mum called.

'There's a whisper that this dog-heart Tony Buttons has people in London,' I said. 'Please tell me it's not true.'

'Kadeen, you been talking to Sienna? You know how she love to exaggerate tings. There is rumour 'pon rumour. There is talk and talk. Try to ignore it. You're safe where you are.'

'OK, me will try.'

'Try to concentrate on school. It's a big day for you tomorrow, and you want to make a good impression.'

'Me nervous,' I admitted. 'The English teachers might tink me stupid.'

'Kadeen Best! Me don't raise no damn fool. You're an intelligent young woman.'

'Can you say that again?' I wanted reassurance.

'Me don't need to tell you again,' Mum said. 'Now, forward to this school and do your best. And don't chat back to any teachers.'

'Me will do my best, Mum.'

I wished Edson was here to help me with any maths homework I might get.

12

Evelyn Grace Academy

I couldn't believe I had to wear grey trousers as part of my school uniform. The only dose of colour I had was the green trimmings on my black blazer and my tie. I had a white shirt and a V-neck pullover. Aunt Mel even pulled out the yellow, green and black beads from my braids.

I looked into the mirror and gazed at a plain reflection of myself. I so wanted to stick a red rose in my hair if I could find one in this grey land.

'Don't England allow any kinda colour?' I protested to Aunt Mel. 'Becah the sky is always grey, do me have to dress like it too?'

'Kadeen, hush your mouth and be glad you're attending school while you're here so in London.'

'But me can't even wear me red trainers.'

'Nobody is allowed to wear trainers,' Aunt Mel confirmed. 'Everybody have to wear black shoes. And *no* big heels.'

'Me hope nobody laugh at me.'

'Why would they laugh at you?' Aunt Mel replied. 'Your mother is always bragging and boasting about your schoolwork. The curriculum at Evelyn Grace is a liccle different from what you're used to in Old Harbour. In history there'll be more focus on British and European history.'

'So nothing about Jamaican heroes like Chief Tacky, Sam Sharpe, Paul Bogle or Queen Nanny of the Maroons? And nothing about the people who were in the Caribbean before the white man come?'

'Me don't tink so. Probably more on English kings and queens and all the wars. You know how the English love to talk about the Second World War. The bulldog spirit and all that. They don't like to talk about how the English went all over the globe to terrorise good people.'

'There is a world history part to the Caribbean Secondary Education Certificate,' I said. 'So me hope what dem teach me, me can put to use.'

'Everyting you learn you can put to use,' Aunt Mel said. 'Now, get your backside outta me yard. Me don't want you late on your first day. Remember to go to reception. You know the way, right?'

'Yes, me tink so.'

*

It felt very strange walking to school and seeing students who were wearing the same uniform as me, but I didn't know any of them.

I slowed down as I approached the gates.

Shall I enter? Maybe me can be like Louella and spend the day in Brockwell Park. Me have me ball and red boots wid me in a bag. And when me get tired of that, me can feed the ducks. But if Mum and Dad found out me wouldn't hear the last of it. They would cuss me till me big toe turn crusty. Aunt Mel would be waiting for me in the afterlife to beat me wid an empty Prosecco bottle.

Me can do this.

I stepped through the gates and made my way to reception.

I introduced myself to a black lady behind the counter. She spoke with an English accent that made me feel nervous. 'We're expecting you, Kadeen,' she said. 'Just wait here for a minute and someone from the English department will come and collect you.'

I sat down in a chair and tapped my feet. I wanted to play keepy-uppy with my ball.

Five minutes later a Ms Campbell arrived to take me to my English class. To add to the icicles in my veins, jelly had replaced my bones. I could hardly put one foot in front of the other.

'You have nothing to worry about, Kadeen,' said Ms Campbell, recognising my anxiety. 'Just concentrate on the school motto. *Excellence, Self-Discipline and Endeavour.* This is a good school.'

I arrived at my English class. There were pictures of famous authors and books on the walls. I recognised the covers of *To Kill a Mockingbird*, *Noughts & Crosses* and *The Hate U Give*.

Ms Campbell spoke quietly to Ms Morgan, the English teacher, as the students all stared at me like I carried my head inside my bag instead of the football.

'Can we give a warm welcome to new student Kadeen Best,' Ms Morgan said. 'She'll be studying with us for a short while.'

I heard two *Hi, Kadeen*s and one *Hello, Kadeen*. The other learners just mumbled and looked the other way. I had never felt so alone in all my years.

Kadeen, remember, you're just as important as anyone else, Edson said to me once.

Kadeen, you can do this.

I found a desk at the back of the class and stared at the floor when I sat down.

Ms Morgan followed me and gave me a copy of a book, *An Inspector Calls* by J.B. Priestley.

Please don't ask me to read, please don't ask me to read, please don't ask me to read.

Thankfully I wasn't asked to perform a reading. I'm not sure if my goo-filled legs would've held me upright, and I'm sure my tongue would've tied itself.

I got through the lesson without embarrassing myself.

Next was maths, where I struggled. It was OK though. Most of my fellow students were also having issues with angles, triangles and logarithm tables.

At break, my phone vibrated. You weren't allowed to bring any mobile phones or devices to school, but I had slipped it into the inside of my blazer pocket. Aunt Mel wouldn't be happy.

I went to the girls' toilets and opened the message.

It was from Sienna.

Kadeen, big tings ah gwaan!

You must watch this.

Me sure one of dem stood in the room when me was interviewed by Officer Myers.

She had attached a video to it. I turned the volume to low and pressed play.

The recording was filmed outside Old Harbour Police Station. Two police officers were in handcuffs being led to a police van that had its hazard lights blinking. Two police motorcyclists were waiting to escort it. A small crowd had assembled near the entrance of the building. Others stood up on boxes and chairs on the High Street. They weren't happy. One of them prepared to fling a sweet potato at the arrested officers. I could just about make out what they chanted.

The Girl With the Red Boots

Traitor! Traitor!
Send dem to firing squad!
Whole heap of police corruption!
Too many police are too damn greedy!
Fling dem into the alligators' pond.

The video only lasted twenty seconds or so. I watched it again because I thought I recognised one of the handcuffed officers.

Yes! He was standing by the door when Officer Myers interviewed me at the police station. Sienna was right. Why has he been arrested? What the flies and lizards is going on?

I texted Mum.

No immediate response.

I had to attend my next lesson: history.

I couldn't concentrate on the Industrial Revolution and factories opening in the north-west of England.

'Kadeen? Everything OK?' Mr Hopgood, my history teacher, asked. 'I know what we are focusing on might be an element of history that is new to you. I'll be happy to go through it with you again, to give you the context. The raw materials were shipped into ports like Liverpool and sent to Manchester and surrounding towns. They manufactured clothes and fabrics on an industrial—'

'No, it's all right, Mr Hopgood,' I interrupted. 'Me know what to do.'

I didn't know what to do. I couldn't rid my mind of the image of two police officers in handcuffs.

What's that all about?

Lunch didn't come quick enough.

Immediately I went to the toilets to text Mum again. Still, no response.

What's wrong wid her? She must know what went down. Me going to call her as soon as me reach home.

My rice and chicken school lunch was just about passable, but nobody had any hot pepper sauce. The meat was tasteless, but I ate it anyway. I made a mental note to bring my own pepper or seasoning in the morning – Aunt Mel had a wide selection. The chocolate sponge pudding was good though. I wasn't used to that dessert in Jamaica.

I went out to a corner in the playground and swapped my black shoes for my red Puma trainers. I took out my ball and played keepy-uppy with my feet and my head.

Focusing on my skills, I tried not to fret about what had been happening at Old Harbour Police Station.

I had made seventeen nods without dropping the ball when a teacher approached. He shook his head and pointed at my red footwear.

I was about to say something, but I kept my thoughts to myself and changed back into my black shoes. They were new so I dared not play keepy-uppy in them.

Maybe grey trainers would be acceptable.

Following lunch, I had an IT lesson. I wasn't as advanced as the others, but I enjoyed it. I sat next to this mix-race girl called Emma. She had a wild afro and a typing speed of a million words a minute. She was tall enough to be a pick for the basketball team. She had a secret stash of Maltesers that she shared with me.

'You're from Jamaica, right?' she asked.

'Yeah, Old Harbour.'

'My dad's from Saint Ann's Bay, Jamaica,' she said. 'Went to visit last summer.'

'He's . . . he's not here wid you?'

'No,' she replied. 'It's a long story.'

Miss Evans, our IT teacher, warned us to be quiet.

'How long are you here for?' Emma whispered.

'Me not too sure,' I replied. 'It's complicated.'

'Your family haven't got their stay yet? My dad's waiting for a visa.'

'No, it's nothing to do with immigration or visas.'

'Then what is it?' Emma wanted to know.

'It will take too long to explain,' I said.

'Emma and . . . is it Kadeen?' Miss Evans raised her voice. 'I'm sure your urgent conversation can wait until after school.'

We went back to our screens, but it was nice to make a new friend, even if Emma was a bit nosy.

As soon as I reached home, I video-called Mum. She didn't pick up, but she returned my call half an hour later. She was in the green room where her television station entertained guests with coffee, juices and fruits before they went on set to be interviewed. I was alone there once and I almost emptied the Diet Coke dispenser. Mum cussed me all the way home for that one.

Mum was backdropped by the yellow, green and purple colours on the wall. I could make out the TV Jamaica logo. She wore her fave black suit with a white blouse.

'Mum!' I asked. 'What's going on? Sienna sent me a video of two handcuffed police officers being taken away from the station. Nuff people were shouting abuse. One man was about to fling a sweet potato at dem.'

'Kadeen, how are you?' Mum replied, avoiding my question. 'How was your first day at school? You did all right? You make any new friends? How were the lessons? Are you getting on OK wid Aunt Mel? She can be a liccle funny sometimes.'

'Mum!'

'Me really don't want to stress you out.'

'Me stressed out already,' I said. 'You might as well tell me becah me will find out eventually.'

'Many tings happened in just one day,' Mum explained. 'Me not too sure where to start.'

Mum usually had two creases in her forehead. Today she had three.

'What kinda tings?'

'First of all, somebody fling a petrol bomb at our front door.'

'A petrol bomb!' I repeated. 'Were you home? Our house burn up? These wolf-hearts are ungodly, me tell you! May The Most High strike dem down and burn dem to a cinder!'

The Girl With the Red Boots

'Kadeen! Watch your language! You never invite death on a fellow human being.'

'Me sorry. Me feelings are rising, me tell you . . . What mash up?'

'There's . . . there's a liccle damage. Me might have to get somebody to scrape off the door and repaint it. Or just get a new door.'

'Who did it?'

Mum turned away from the camera.

'Me can't hear you too good, Kadeen,' Mum said. 'Your voice is breaking up. Bad connection. Let me move to the table. It's usually better there.'

Mum sat down at a round table. There was a bowl of fruit sitting on there, full of bananas, oranges, mangoes, avocados and red grapes.

Me could die for a fresh mango right now. I licked my lips.

I recognised weather girl Wendy Walton in her yellow, green and purple trouser suit sitting opposite Mum. Edson once boasted she had kissed him on the cheek when he was at the station on work experience. He didn't wash his face for days. She was reading a fashion magazine. She was pretty enough to be in it.

'Who firebombed our house, Mum?'

'They tink it a somebody connected to Tony Buttons.'

'Dem get arrested?'

'Afraid not,' Mum replied. 'One of our neighbours reported it. Dem drive off in a white car, fast like they just robbed a bank.'

'How did they know where we live?'

I heard Mum take a breath. She closed her eyes for a short second. 'They had inside information. Two people on the inside at Old Harbour Police Station. Clive Hibbert and Vincent Daly. Dem go through the messages and voicemails on their phones. Their bank statements show a big amount of credit that wasn't paid by the police. None of dem had any explanation for it. They have been taken to a secure place in Kingston for further questioning.'

'Clive Hibbert?' I repeated. 'Wasn't he the man who was in the room when Officer Myers take me statement?'

Moment of silence.

'Mum? Was he?'

'Yes, he was,' Mum confirmed. 'The commander called me in person and sent his apologies. He realised that we were all put in danger. He promised to refund any costs for any damage to our property.'

'But, Mum,' I interrupted. 'If dem know where me live in Old Harbour, they might know where me there in London.'

'Me been assured that Clive Hibbert and Vincent Daly didn't have access to that information. Only Crystal Myers and her commanding officer know. Crystal swore on that.'

'You sure?'

'That's what dem tell me, Kadeen. Just stay where you are. Jamaica is too dangerous for you right now. As me say to you before, don't do anyting to bring attention to

The Girl With the Red Boots

yourself. Keep a low profile. Obviously Tony Buttons and his nasty people want to intimidate us.'

'When . . . when do you think me can return home?'

'Me don't know, Kadeen,' Mum replied. 'Me not even sure when me can return to the house. I have to arrange a time when me can take the rest of the clothes and valuables out of the house. Me don't drive to work any more. My boss sends me a taxi every morning. Him don't want me car to get recognise.'

'We should not be living like this, Mum. What are the police doing? Edson been dead for weeks and weeks now. Dem still have no idea where this devil man Tony Buttons is.'

'The police in America are looking for him,' Mum said. 'Me don't tink he'll be able to board another plane. The Florida state police and the FBI have him profile all over.'

'You tink he might make his way somehow back to Jamaica? Maybe by boat?'

'The truth is, nobody knows.'

Mum dropped her head. She stared at the table. She looked up again after a short while and tried to hide her concern. 'Kadeen, hear me good,' she said. 'This Tony Buttons or his gang will not destroy our family. You hear me? We're going to keep on doing what we always do. We can't be together right now but on one fine day we will. Believe that.'

'Me . . . me believe it, Mum.'

'Good, try not to fret. Work hard at school and don't play your ball in Mel's yard.'
'OK, Mum. We'll talk soon.'
'We will, and don't forget to call your father.'
'Love you, Mum.'
'Me love you too.'

13

Battersea Park

The next morning, Aunt Mel cooked me fried dumplings, ackee, salted cod fish and spinach. She even mixed me a banana, blackberry and strawberry smoothie. Aunt Mel said she would've added mango but they didn't look too ripe in Brixton Market. Late last night I overheard her speaking to Mum. I guessed she wanted to try and make me feel better. I closed my eyes and imagined I was eating breakfast on my home veranda. It was a shame I couldn't feel the rays of a rising Jamaican sun.

'It's a good ting you and your mother moved out,' she said. 'It could have been worse wid that firebomb business. Trust me, Kadeen, you'll be safe here so. Just don't do anyting to get attention like sign up for the next series of *Big Brother* or kiss a royal on a walkabout.'

Battersea Park

I laughed for the first time in days. 'As if me would do anyting like that.'

'Kadeen, me was joking. Just keep on doing your schoolwork, stay outta trouble and come straight home when school done. Me don't want you messing wid dem young people who always crowd around McDonald's and KFC. Sometimes fussing and fighting kick off in there.'

The next day, Emma invited me to stop by KFC on the way home from school. It was ram-jammed with students not just from where I studied but other schools too. We both went for two-piece chicken and fries and found a corner table. They didn't serve smoothies, so I had to make do with a medium Diet Coke. In a back corner of my mind, I realised I was going against Aunt Mel's wishes.

It's not a big ting. Me just going to munch on food and then go back to me yard. Aunt Mel don't have to know.

'Are you going to come with me to club on Wednesday after school?' Emma asked.

'What kinda club?' I asked. 'Basketball?'

Emma laughed. I wondered what the joke was.

'Basketball?' she repeated. 'I'm to basketball like a Sumo wrestler is to ballet. I can hardly catch the ball, let alone throw it.'

'Then what club?' I pressed.

'Chess club,' Emma replied. 'My dad taught me when I was on holiday in Jamaica. I got hooked on the game after watching *The Queen's Gambit* on Netflix.'

The Girl With the Red Boots

'The Queen's what? Sounds nasty.'

'It's not nasty,' Emma assured me. 'It's about a girl who's hot at chess. My mum loved it too.'

'Your . . . your mum's white, right?'

'Yeah.'

'How did your parents meet?' I asked.

For a short second, I wondered if it was an appropriate question. I had only known Emma for a few days.

'Mum flew out to Jamaica on holiday with her workmates,' Emma replied. 'She's a nurse at King's College Hospital working in the children's ward. She stayed at the Riu Hotel in Ocho Rios on a package deal. My dad was working there at the time as part of the entertainment team. He did all the swimming-pool and dancing activities. They got together one night over strawberry daiquiris.'

'What's a strawberry daiquiri?' I wondered.

'A rum cocktail with a dose of strawberry. One thing led to another and that's why I'm sitting with you sinking fried chicken.'

We both laughed.

'Four years ago, I stayed at the same hotel,' Emma went on. 'Dad took us to Dunn's River Falls, the zip ride and swimming with the dolphins. He then drove us to Negril. Those beaches are proper long and the sea is so clean! I just had to have a dip.'

'Of course,' I said. 'You can't go to Negril without swimming in the sea.'

'I met Dad's family,' Emma went on. 'They lived in Saint

Ann's Bay. My grandma cooked up a wicked dish of curried goat with so much vegetables and rice, I had to sit down for days to digest it all. I love Jamaica.'

I thought about my family and friends back home. Edson gatecrashed my thoughts. He loved to chargrill sausages, burgers and chicken wings at family functions. There he was in his black Puma baseball cap and brown apron.

'Sis,' he would say. 'Bring come the barbecue sauce! Here's your chicken wings served by the prince of the grill!'

'Me love it too,' I finally replied.

'So, Kadeen, what about the chess thing? We have club on Mondays and Wednesdays after school.'

'Me would love to learn how to play chess, but me might ask if I can go to football practice on a Wednesday evening. There's this local team. The SW2s.'

'Maybe you can come on Mondays or round to mine on any other evening. I will teach you there?'

'Me good wid that,' I said. 'Thank you.'

We finished our fast-food snack and trekked our way up Brixton Hill. Emma lived a few blocks from me on Endymion Road.

As I turned into Josephine Avenue, an idea licked my creative vein.

Aunt Mel had left out two chicken breast fillets to defrost. I washed them and seasoned them before placing them in the oven. I boiled a pot of rice and steamed cauliflower and green beans.

After the chicken me have today, me going to look like ah rooster!

Arriving home just after 5.30 p.m., Aunt Mel was well happy that I had cooked for her.

We sat down to eat.

'I'm joining the school chess club on Wednesdays after school,' I announced.

'Kadeen, me never know you can play chess,' Aunt Mel replied.

'Me can't,' I said. 'But me will learn.'

'I guess playing chess won't bring too much attention like football or basketball,' Aunt Mel said. She paused for a moment, as though she was thinking of a nice memory. 'It will take your mind off tings. You'll make new friends.'

'Don't expect me home till after seven,' I said.

'After seven?' Aunt Mel repeated. 'That's a long time playing chess.'

'The members usually go for a soft drink and a snack after the club,' I lied. 'Me want to go wid dem. You did say me should try and make friends while me here.'

Aunt Mel side-eyed me. 'All right.' She nodded. 'But no later than seven. And don't bother get crazy wid the soft drink. It's bad for your teeth. You hear me? Your mother tell me about your great love for Coca-Cola.'

'Me hear you good.'

Battersea Park

I felt bad about lying to Aunt Mel, but I didn't think she'd ever allow me to play football.

Louella texted me the next morning. She said it was OK for me to train with the SW2s. She told me to wait outside some place called the Hootananny on Effra Road. I'd be picked up there on Wednesday at 5 p.m.

What the bullfrogs and cockroaches is the Hootananny? It sounds like an ancient owl. In England they have plenty strange names.

Aunt Mel usually arrived home from work around 5.30 p.m., so I had time to reach home after school and pick up my red boots and tracksuit.

It turned out the Hootananny was a pub and live-music venue. A poster advertised a Brixtongue live reading event.

Me wonder what that's all about? Maybe dem play a liccle dancehall music in there. Me miss the reggae playing everywhere in Old Harbour.

I was picked up by a blue Mini. Louella sat in the front passenger seat. The driver was this heavy-set lady wearing a grey tracksuit and she had a whistle on a string around her neck. She looked about fifty-ish. Her brown hair was pulled back into a ponytail. She owned a pair of harsh eyebrows and chubby cheeks. She had a mini football dangling from her rear mirror.

'This is Sonia,' Louella introduced us. 'Ms Sonia Francis. She's our coach.'

The car stank of cats and beer.

The Girl With the Red Boots

'Nice to meet you,' I managed.

'Hi, Kadeen,' Sonia greeted me. 'Please refer to me as Miss Francis or Coach Francis.'

As I climbed into the back seat, I glanced at Miss Francis and thought of the wrestling shows that Edson loved to watch.

I shared my seat with red cones, footballs, random pieces of footwear and cat hair. I sneezed a mega sneeze.

'Have you played for a team before?' Miss Francis asked.

'Not really,' I replied. 'Me brother Edson played for a team back in Jamaica and sometimes me would join the training.'

'Do you have your own boots?'

'Yes,' I replied. 'Red Puma. Me pride and joy. Me brother bought me dem.'

'OK,' Coach Francis said. 'We shall see how good you are.'

I felt anxious as Miss Francis reversed her Mini into a parking bay at Battersea Park. I helped carry cones to the training pitches before we got into our kit in the changing rooms.

Eleven players, including me, had turned up for the session. They all seemed taller and broader than me.

'At fourteen,' Louella said, 'me and you are the youngest players here.'

I was introduced to the team.

'Blanka Tomaszewski is our crazy goalkeeper from

Poland,' Coach Francis started with a grin. 'You already know Louella; no one gets past her in a rush. Bernice and Dionne play centre defence and Zoe plays left back.'

Bernice and Dionne were tall enough to bounce ball with the LA Lakers.

'Maria is our central midfielder,' Coach Francis continued. 'She's from Seville, Spain, and we call her Sleeping Boots. If we win the league this year, she's promised to take us all back to her homeland to watch a bullfight and eat fresh oranges.'

'Why do you call her Sleeping Boots?' I wanted to know.

Everyone laughed. 'You'll get to know soon enough,' Coach Francis replied. 'Hee Yan is our defensive midfield player. She covers our back four like a terrier protecting its bone. Neesha and Paula are our wide midfielders. Yolanda plays up front and Tracey . . .'

Coach Francis paused to scan the changing room. She then checked her watch. 'Tracey's late again!' She raised her voice. 'I absolutely hate lateness. And if you're late twice in a row, you'll not be playing. I don't care if I can't field eleven players or if you scored a hat-trick last week. Do you understand that rule, Kadeen?'

'Er, yes.' I nodded. 'Me understand.'

'OK,' said Coach Francis. 'Let's go and warm up.'

'Let's do it!' roared Blanka. She struck a pose and tensed her biceps like she was about to duel to the death with a *Game of Thrones* villain.

Maybe she does wrestling too?

The Girl With the Red Boots

Coach Francis handed me a yellow bib to pull over my tracksuit top and led us out to the floodlit artificial pitch. She supervised stretches and jogging. I was impressed that she performed every exercise she asked the players to do. The cold in the air bit my cheeks, neck and fingers.

Should've worn gloves. Wait a minute. Me don't own any.

Coach Francis split us into two teams of six – the yellow bibs against the sky-blue bibs. She placed cones eight paces apart for the goals, and she played goalkeeper for my team, the yellows. I was thankful I didn't have to play against Louella and her crunching tackles.

'I want you to concentrate on keeping the ball,' Coach Francis instructed. 'Pass and move, pass and move.'

As Coach Francis blew her whistle to start the game, nerves licked my bloodstream, or my bloodstream kicked my nerves. I couldn't tell.

I mis-controlled the ball the first time I received it.

'Get the basics right!' Coach Francis yelled. 'Pass and move, find space. Keep your head up.'

The next time I got the ball, I confronted Zoe with it. I tried a body feint and dribble past her. She stuck out a left foot and I lost possession. My confidence ran away from me.

'Chase back! Chase back!' Coach Francis barked. 'Don't let your head drop.'

I raced after shadows for the next ten minutes. Maria, aka Sleeping Boots, had all the skills. She could dribble, pass and score goals. I just couldn't get involved in the game. I tried to imagine I was playing with Edson. Carefree football, he called it. *Enjoy the game.*

Coach Francis hurled the ball to me after she caught it from a corner. I had a bit of space to work in. Zoe sprinted to defend against me. I feinted to go to her outside but flicked the ball to my left. I sprinted past her. Dionne was next. I decided to take her on the outside. I accelerated around her. Tall defenders are like aircraft carriers, slow to turn. The angle to the goal was acute, but I tried a right foot shot. It struck the red cone, causing it to tumble over.

'No faluking way you're beating me from there,' Blanka roared.

'Unlucky, Kadeen,' Louella yelled encouragement.

Yolanda threw her arms up in the air. 'I was unmarked,' she hollered. 'Pass the friggin' ball. Didn't you see me? I had an open goal.'

'Sorry, I didn't see you,' I replied.

'It might help if you open your eyes,' Yolanda spat back.

'Keep it civil,' Coach Francis warned. 'Keep it calm. Remember, you're teammates.'

Yolanda side-eyed me like she wanted to lick me with a red cone.

Two minutes later, my team built another attack. I was played in on the right-hand side of the penalty area. I attempted another shot. Blanka saved easily. '*Nie ma problemu,*' she yelled in Polish.

I remembered Edson's words when I missed an opportunity.

The Girl With the Red Boots

Is that all you've got, Kadeen? Me invited you to play in a boys' game and you miss an open goal? Come, sis, you can do better than that.

I sucked in a long breath and steeled myself.

Don't let your head drop. Me will show dem!

The next time I received the ball, I faced my own goal. I dummied to go to my left before spinning around and darting to my right. One defender passed. Hee Yan was next. I attacked her at speed and nutmegged her. Only Blanka to beat. 'You think you can score against me!' She rushed out to challenge me like she was a line-backer in American football.

Lord ah mercy! Me might get crushed and paralysed here so.

Yolanda screamed for a pass. I could see a gap to the left side of the goal. I went for it. Blanka dived and managed to get a left palm to it. The ball hit the red cone and rolled across the goal-line before Yolanda tapped it over.

Goal!

Coach Francis blew her whistle. She marched up to me like I had strangled one of her cats.

What's wid her?

Coach Francis huffed and puffed until she got right up close to me. Her cheeks were red and her hands were on her hips. She shook her head as her eyes locked into mine.

'Kadeen,' she said. 'If I remember rightly, this is a six-a-side game. *Not* one against six. Even the best players in the world pass to a teammate if they're in a better position to score a goal. Do you understand?'

I stared at the ground. 'Yes,' I replied. 'Me sorry.'

I glanced at Yolanda. She clapped. 'Tell her, Coach Francis.'

'Don't be sorry,' Coach Francis said. 'My job is to make you a better player, a team player.'

'OK.' I nodded.

'When you dribble or run at speed with the ball,' she went on, 'try and lift your head up and see where your teammates are.'

'Me will try me best.'

'You have great speed, Kadeen.' Coach Francis smiled. 'And some wonderful skills. But remember, it's a team game.'

Coach Francis jogged back to her goal and blew her whistle to restart the game.

'Come on!' Blanka roared as she took a goal kick. 'Brutalise them! Pulverise them! Mash them like a soft potato.'

Five minutes later, I managed to find Yolanda with a pass and she scored a well-taken goal. I turned around to check Coach Francis' response and she clapped me. She then gave me a thumbs up. '*Don't* admire your pretty work,' she shouted. 'Time to defend. Concentrate.'

Coach Francis blew her final whistle at 6.45 p.m. I fretted about reaching home before seven.

I helped carry the cones to Coach Francis' Mini as she

offered advice. 'Even the great Brazilian team of 1970 played as a team,' she said. 'Of course, they had wonderful individual players like Pelé, Rivellino, Jairzinho and Carlos Alberto. They had all the skills in the world. But if you watch the last goal they scored in the final, it was pure teamwork.'

'1970?' I repeated. 'That's ancient times. Not even my mum was alive then. Did you watch it live?'

'I'm giving away my age here.' Coach Francis grinned. 'Yes. I was nine years old and watched it on a tiny black-and-white TV in a small terraced house in Balham. We had to stand on a chair and tweak the aerial to get a decent picture. Been hooked on football ever since.'

'So . . . that make you . . . over sixty?'

'Nothing wrong with your maths, Kadeen.'

'If Tracey doesn't turn up,' Louella said. 'Will you play Kadeen in her place?'

'We'll see,' Coach Francis replied. 'We'll see. I'll give Tracey a buzz tonight. I'll find out what happened to her. Right, hop in the car, I've gotta get back and feed my cats.'

Coach Francis dropped me off outside my flat fifteen minutes later. It was 7.15 p.m. I wiped off a blob of mud that had stuck on my tracksuit top, took a deep breath and turned my key in the front door.

'Is that you, Kadeen?' Aunt Mel asked from the kitchen. 'You must be hungry. I cooked some salmon fillets, pasta and broccoli.'

Battersea Park

'Thank you, Aunt Mel. Me just going to drop off me bag and me will be wid you.'

I quickly decided to wash my red boots in the morning when Aunt Mel had left for work. I wanted to confess to her about my football.

But what if she bans me from playing? Me really enjoyed training this evening.

'So how did you find chess club?' Aunt Mel asked as I sat at the kitchen table. She sipped from a glass of white wine.

'Oh, it's a complex game,' I said.

'Yes, well complex but good for your brain. It's all about strategy. You learn all the moves of the pieces?'

'Not . . . not all of dem. Me . . . me just watch for a while.'

'And you make any new friends?' Aunt Mel wanted to know.

'Yes, me good friends wid this mix-race girl call Emma. She live on Endymion Road. Her dad is Jamaican.'

'That's nice,' Aunt Mel said as she placed my plate in front of me. Aunt Mel also set down a jar of homemade tartare sauce. It was super-duper delicious. She poured me a glass of orange juice. 'Your mother says you love Coca-Cola too much so me going to juice you up.'

'Not even Coca-Cola on a Sunday?'

'Hmmmm. Me suppose so. But only one glass.'

'Thank you,' I replied. 'You been very good to me since me reach here so.'

The Girl With the Red Boots

Guilt licked me hard in my stomach and my head.

Maybe me should tell her. Me can't take this deception for much longer. Edson wouldn't like it either. I smashed a neighbour's window once with a stray shot. Nobody but Edson had witnessed it. 'Better to confess,' he said. 'Otherwise, guilt will mash up your conscience.'

I confessed and Edson helped me pay the bill.

14

Montego Bay

Aunt Mel wanted me in my bed by ten, but before I turned in, I watched YouTube highlights of the great Brazil team that won the 1970 World Cup. Pelé was incredible. Jairzinho, Rivellino and Carlos Alberto too. Coach Francis wasn't wrong, the last goal they scored in the final was from a simple pass by Pelé. The whole move was like a choreographed dance. Football heaven. *Delishi-ocious.*

It was just after eleven. I decided to call Dad.

'Kadeen! Lovely to hear from you. How are you?'

'Me good, Dad. Me start at this school call Evelyn Grace Academy, me make a few friends and me getting on good wid Aunt Mel.'

'That's good, that's good.'

'The only ting is, England cold like polar-bear sneeze. The coldness goes right through you. Me could wear ten tracksuits at the same time, and the chill will still get through. Believe it!'

'Too cold to play football?' Dad asked.

'You must warm up first,' I said. 'Get your blood running in your system again.'

'Aunt Mel let you play?'

How do me respond to this? Me don't want to lie to me dad.

'Sort of,' I replied.

'What do you mean sort of?' Dad pressed.

'Me don't tell her yet.'

'Kadeen! What do you mean you don't tell her yet?'

'She might ban me from playing,' I reasoned.

'She might not. She might be understanding. Although she had an experience when she was a teenager.'

'Yes, me hear someting about that a few years ago? Mum did touch on it one time, but when me enter the room, she wouldn't say any more. Do you know what it is?'

'That's for her to tell you,' Dad replied. 'Me can't reveal it.'

'Can't you give me a clue?'

'All me can say,' Dad said, 'that it was traumatic. It's why she's very cautious about certain tings.'

'Football?'

'Not just football. Any kind of sport event.'

'Me don't know why nobody can tell me,' I said. 'Me not a child any more.'

'It's not for me to say,' replied Dad.

'Anyway. Me found a team to play for, the SW2s. Me

making new friends. Me don't want Aunt Mel to mash it up.'

'You're going to have to tell her sooner or later,' Dad warned. 'You can't carry on wid this lie.'

We fell silent for the next few moments. Dad was right, deceiving Aunt Mel bruised my conscience.

I wanted to change the subject.

'What's going on in Montego Bay?' I asked.

'You don't hear?'

'Hear what?' I wondered.

'There is a curfew,' Dad explained. 'The gang ting is getting outta control. Three people were shot dead the other day in broad daylight. They don't even bother to wait for nightfall to start the shooting. The police order a curfew in downtown Montego Bay. Tourists have been told not to stray from their hotels and be back inside before dark. It's a terrible shame. People will stop visiting our island. Instead, they will go to holiday destinations like Cancún, Dominica or Barbados.'

I couldn't help but think of Edson. His passing hit me hard yet again. His smile. His encouragement.

Perhaps if there had been a curfew in Old Harbour, he'd still be alive.

'Maybe it was a good idea not to stay wid you,' I said.

'Yes, we love you staying wid us, Kadeen, but you're right.'

'How is Monica and Simone?'

'Becah of the violent situation in Montego Bay, Monica

is now looking for a job in Ocho Rios. It's safer there. Simone is all right. When you're that age, the stress of living don't touch you.'

'Give her a hug from me.'

'Me will,' Dad replied. 'But talk to Aunt Mel. It's not good lying to her. We never raise you that way. You must trust her. And if your mother finds out? Well, you know how she can cuss badword when she ready.'

'Yes, me know. Bye, Dad. Walk and drive safe.'

'And you keep safe too. Love you, Kadeen.'

I killed the call, stretched out on my bed and wondered how the crabs and oysters I was going to tell Aunt Mel that I had been lying to her.

What happened in her teenage years that no one wants to talk about?

15

Strategy

Two days later, I stepped up Brixton Hill with Emma, following school. I still felt guilty I hadn't told Aunt Mel that I had joined a football club.

'Would it be easier if I was with you when you told her?' offered Emma.

I shook my head. 'That might make it a whole heap worse.'

'You're gonna have to tell her before she finds out.'

I thought about it and walked on another few paces. 'Me will tell her on Sunday. We have a game so me can't really get out of it.'

'Just tell her it's a way of making new friends,' suggested Emma.

'Yeah, good idea. Me not lying. Me still need to learn chess though.'

The Girl With the Red Boots

'Why don't you come up to my place,' said Emma. 'Mum don't finish work till seven today. I'll teach you some chess moves after our homework.'

'Homework?' I repeated. 'Me forget about that. Me have some history to do.'

'And I've got biology,' groaned Emma.

Emma lived in a first-floor flat in a town house. I had yet to see a bungalow in Brixton like my own back home. Emma's open-plan lounge and kitchen had bay windows that looked out to the street. A cream-coloured leather sofa sat against a wall with a matching footstool in front of it.

A glass coffee table with chrome legs had Jamaican souvenir coasters placed in each of its corners.

There was a framed poster of the movie *Dancehall Queen* hanging from a wall next to a similar image of *Dirty Dancing*.

In the kitchen, souvenir magnets from Morocco, Cyprus, Croatia and Jamaica niced up the fridge. Resting on a shelf was an unopened bottle of Captain Morgan's Spiced Rum and a little koala bear cuddly toy. There were two framed photographs of Emma and her mum and dad playing on a beach.

Edson and me will never play ball on the sands of Old Harbour Bay again.

I shook my head to try and shake my sadness away.

Emma switched on the TV and asked Alexa to play Afrobeat music. She turned the volume down low so we could concentrate on our homework.

In history class we studied the Battle of the Somme from

Strategy

the First World War. It was hard for me to comprehend that 19,240 poor souls had been killed on the first day of that conflict.

Oh, my gosh! How is that even possible?

My essay focused on why the military commanders had allowed such a devastating death toll to be acceptable. *Because they were too damn stupid, and lives were cheap,* I wanted to write.

I was glad when I heard Emma say she had finished her work.

I snapped my book shut and Emma sat beside me. 'Can I ask you something personal?' she asked.

'Yes, course. Go for it.'

'Sometimes,' Emma started. 'Sometimes, when you're thinking that no one's looking, I look at you and you seem soooo sad. What's going on?'

'Er . . . what do you mean?'

'It's like you're miles away,' Emma added. 'Living through your worst life.'

I stared at the floor. Emma had a light-brown carpet that had enjoyed better days but I couldn't spot any grime in it.

'Kadeen?'

'Sorry . . . just tinking,' I replied. 'You're right . . . Me . . . me lost me brother a few weeks ago. Edson was his name. He was shot dead in my hometown square. Me . . . me hear the gunshot on me way home from school. Me miss him every day . . . every hour. He was a great brother to me.'

Emma covered her mouth. 'Oh . . . I didn't mean . . . you know. Sorry for your loss. That's just . . . horrible. There . . . there was a girl in our year at school who lost her older brother to knife crime. It devastated everyone. We had assemblies about it.'

I told Emma the whole story from when I left school that fateful day until I went to my bed that night still expecting Edson to arrive home. I couldn't stem the tears.

Emma gave me a warm hug. 'So until they catch this . . .'

'Tony Buttons,' I reminded Emma.

'You'll be here in the UK,' said Emma. 'Gosh, I can't imagine what it would be like if I had to leave my home cos someone killed my brother. It's just terrible.'

'Please don't say anyting to anybody at school,' I pleaded. 'Only the headmaster is supposed to know. Me meant to be keeping a low profile.'

'My lips are zipped on that one,' promised Emma. She pointed to her mouth. 'Nothing's spilling from here.'

'Me trust you,' I said.

'If . . . if you wanna talk . . . about anything,' Emma said. 'Then I'm here. I'm . . . I'm just so sorry.'

I smiled. My heart felt warm as I embraced my new friend once more.

'My dad's been trying to get a visa for years,' Emma said. 'Don't know why the Home Office won't give him a permanent stay. He's a banging dancer. He can write and act too. They didn't mind letting in so many Ukrainians.'

'Your pops ever been to the UK?' I asked.

Strategy

'He has,' Emma replied. 'But only on a holiday visa. He can only stay up to two or three months.'

'Do you miss him?' I asked.

Emma nodded. 'Yeah, he calls me his liccle princess. He shows me all the latest Jamaican dance moves. He wants to start a career in entertainment, but if he can't do that, maybe a position in the media.'

I thought of my dad, and the day he left our family home. Mum didn't say a word that day. Instead, she busied herself in housework. I sat in my room staring at the walls in disbelief. I heard Dad zip up his suitcase and place his belongings in cardboard boxes. I remember Edson and me kicking a ball to each other after he drove away. I couldn't sleep that night. I half expected him to come home in the early hours of the morning. He usually sank his ackee and fried dumpling breakfast and drank his mango juice sitting on his high bar stool. Nobody filled that seat for the longest time.

Since then, Dad had always been a presence in my life. I felt lucky because a few of my friends had never met theirs.

'Time for chess,' Emma said.

She went to her bedroom and returned with a chess set. She cleared the coffee table, opened the board and set the black and white wooden pieces into their positions. She held up a pawn and proceeded to teach me its movements. She then moved on to the horse.

'It's a knight,' Emma corrected me.

'But it looks like a horse,' I argued. 'Why call it a knight and make it look like a horse?'

'Just pretend a knight is sitting on the horse with a sword in his hand.'

'Does it have to be a "he"?' I wondered.

Emma giggled as she showed me how the knight moved. 'You're right, it doesn't have to be a "he".'

Another half-hour of chess and a hot chocolate later, Emma walked me to her front door.

'Your aunt doesn't seem too bad,' she said. 'Just be honest with her. I'm sure she'll be OK with you playing football.'

'OK.' I nodded. 'Me will tell her this evening. Hopefully, me punishment won't be too bad.'

16

Promotion

I reached home just after 5.45 p.m.

Aunt Mel hadn't arrived yet, so I took the opportunity to sweep and mop the kitchen floor, vacuum the hallway and run a cleaning cloth over the furniture in the lounge. I sprayed lavender air freshener to sweeten up the place. I wanted to be in Aunt Mel's top ratings before my confession.

She finally reached home just after half-six. I smiled at her as she entered the kitchen, but she didn't acknowledge me as she closed her umbrella and pulled off her raincoat. 'Blasted, ignorant people!' she shouted.

She placed a brown paper bag of takeaway food on the kitchen table. 'Not cooking tonight,' she announced. 'So me get a liccle someting from the Satay Bar. Some noodles and ting.'

The Girl With the Red Boots

'Thank you,' I said.

She opened the fridge and reached for her bottle of white wine. 'Sometimes you don't get the appreciation you deserve,' she said. 'No, sah!'

She poured herself a full glass, splashing a few drops on the table. She tipped her head back and gave herself a generous sip. She then licked her lips. 'Blasted, ignorant, unappreciative people, dem!'

'Every . . . everyting all right?' I asked.

When she replied, she didn't look at me. 'Not really,' she said. 'Go and eat your food, Kadeen. It's roasted Thai chicken wid veg and noodles.'

We ate our dinner in silence. I really enjoyed the spiciness of the chicken and the sauces. Aunt Mel pushed her food around with her fork as she rested her head into her left palm. She stared absently through the window.

'What's . . . what's up?' I tried again. 'If looks could kill, the plants in the yard woulda dead long time.'

Aunt Mel half grinned. She topped off her wine glass before she looked at me. 'I've been working at that damn place for nearly twenty years and yet me see people get promoted before me. People who me train up! Now me have to call dem manager!'

'Sorry to hear,' I managed.

'And me never go sick,' Aunt Mel went on. '*Never* . . . No, me tell a lie. Apart from me operation, where me take off a week. But me never take a whole heap of time off like others do.'

Promotion

'Operation?' I repeated.

'Yes, your mother knows.' Aunt Mel side-eyed me. 'It's a woman ting. Someting was causing my heavy periods. Endometriosis, they call it. Don't ask me to spell it. Me had to have an operation down below. Very painful.'

'Oh,' I said. 'Me sorry to hear.'

'And when other people take time off for sickness, me cover for dem, do twice the work but when it come to promotion, dem don't see me! Blasted, ignorant, foolish people, dem! If it wasn't for my age, I'd give dem me notice.'

'Maybe . . . maybe next time,' I suggested.

Aunt Mel offered me the look from hell. 'Next time! Next time? Do you know how many next times there have been since me work at that damn place?'

She kissed her teeth, picked up her bottle of wine and glass and headed for her bedroom. She slammed the door shut. The doorframe shook.

Maybe not the best time to tell her about the football ting right now.

I finished my dinner, found a bottle of Coca-Cola in the fridge and poured myself a huge glass. I couldn't help myself.

I switched on the TV to catch the early evening news. Usually Aunt Mel would never miss the local news, but she failed to emerge from her bedroom.

What do me do? Shall me tell her about the football ting? Better not, she vex already, and when me done tell her, she might reach for a next bottle of wine. And then she'll call me mother to tell her what a lying, conniving daughter she have. Maybe leave it for tomorrow . . . or the next day.

I went to bed but as my head hit the pillow, I fretted about Aunt Mel. I decided to check in on her.

She was lying face-down on her bed still in her work clothes. Her shoes were still on her feet and she snored a mighty snore. I pulled off her footwear, found a pink blanket from her wardrobe and spread it over her. The bottle of wine was three-quarters empty. For a few moments I watched her, recognising that she was going through a hard time now. Before I left, I kissed her on the forehead.

17

SW2s v Dulwich Dames

Sunday had arrived and I still hadn't confessed to Aunt Mel about my football plans. Even worse, I told her on Saturday afternoon that I'd be going around to Emma's Sunday morning to hang out and complete a bit of homework. Guilt totally nagged me, and I could barely catch Aunt Mel's gaze.

'You must tell Emma to come visit we one good day,' Aunt Mel said. 'It'll be nice to meet her. Me will cook someting nice. Maybe some rice and peas, oxtail with butter beans and salad.'

I felt a stab of guilt in my gut.

I had already filled my rucksack with my red football boots and a tub of Vaseline. Bad vibes rumbled in my stomach. I justified to myself that Aunt Mel didn't need any more drama right now.

The Girl With the Red Boots

Coach Francis and Louella picked me up outside the Hootananny. The cat stench in the back seat of her car hadn't improved. Despite the cold, I wound down the window.

'Where are we playing?' I asked.

'The Dulwich ground on the South Circular,' replied Coach Francis. 'Not far from the famous Dulwich College school. It's an away game. Changing rooms are decent there. I heard a rumour that hot water actually comes out of the showers. The pitches are top quality. No slopes, mud heaps or massive puddles that we sometimes have to play in.'

'Famous Dulwich College?' I repeated.

'Oh, yes.' Louella nodded. 'You've got to have a shopping bag full of credit to attend there.'

'Who are we playing again?' I wanted to know.

'The Dames,' replied Louella. 'Their official name is Dulwich Ladies, but everyone calls them the Dames.'

'Why do you call dem the Dames?'

'Because they go on too stoosh,' replied Louella.

'Stoosh?' I repeated.

'Like they're better than everybody else,' Coach Francis explained. 'They've got a fancy air-conditioned van to ride to away games. They've got show-off tracksuits with their names on the backs. In their support team they have a trained masseur and a nutritional advisor. And that's why I enjoy beating them.'

'Me would love to beat dem too,' I said.

SW2s v Dulwich Dames

Coach Francis smiled and handed me a registration form to fill in. 'I should've asked you to fill this in on Wednesday,' she said. 'But later on this evening I'm going to whizz up to the league secretary's office and drop it off.'

'OK,' I said.

I hesitated for a long moment before I started to fill it in.

We arrived at the Dulwich ground and found five of my teammates in the changing room. Blanka had already changed into her goalkeeper's kit and went through her range of stretches. Dionne and Bernice adjusted their socks and tied their boots. Paula placed a hairband around her head and Maria was stretched out along a bench, sleeping.

Ah, that's why they call her Sleeping Boots.

Minutes later, Zoe, Neesha, Hee Yan, Paula and Yolanda arrived. For a moment, I got excited about starting the game but this pretty brown-skin girl with long braids entered the dressing room. She bopped her head to whatever she listened to on her fat headphones. She chewed gum liked a hyena munching a rabbit.

'Me reach!' Tracey hollered.

Everyone held out their hand for a high-five.

'You get changed too, Kadeen,' Coach Francis instructed me. 'I'll definitely be putting you on. Maybe at half-time if we need to chase the game, but probably sometime in the second half. We'll see how we go.'

I felt a rush of adrenaline flowing through me. I quickly

pulled on my kit: green shirt, yellow shorts and black socks, applied Vaseline to my thighs and laced up my red boots.

Me two good red friends. It's been a while.

'Time for action,' I whispered to my footwear. 'Don't let me down.'

'No shin pads?' Coach Francis asked.

I shook my head.

'You can't play without shin pads,' Coach Francis insisted.

She pulled out a pair of leg-guards from a bag of footballs. 'I always bring a spare pair just in case.' Coach Francis grinned. 'But make sure you bring your own, OK, Kadeen?'

By the time I secured my shin protection, Coach Francis invited everyone to join the huddle. I squeezed myself between Blanka and Yolanda.

'Zoe, watch their right winger, she's a bit nippy,' Coach Francis instructed. 'Don't give her too much room. Tackle her hard. Let her know you're there. Get in her face. Their centre forward is a bit slow but she's good in the air so don't allow too many crosses into our box. Their keeper's not as springy on her feet as one of my cats, so test her out with lots of shots, OK? Make her work for her doughnuts.'

'Let's pulverise them!' Blanka roared. 'Destroy them! Mash them like potato! We are the SW2s! And we haven't come here to lose!'

SW2s v Dulwich Dames

As the huddle broke, everyone high-fived each other. It felt nice to be part of something.

I'm an SW2! Just wish Edson could be watching me.

Blanka led us out on to the pitch. The Vaseline I had spread on my legs didn't stop the sudden chill hitting me. I was a substitute, so I went back to the changing rooms to put on my tracksuit.

The pitch was nice and level. The grass had been recently shaved, the goals had nets, and flags stuck out at the four corners. I joined my team in their stretches and warm-up play, and as the referee blew her whistle to start the game, I guessed there were around thirty to forty people watching from the sidelines.

It was a tough game. Our best creative player, Maria, struggled to control the flow. The Dames had a tough-tackling midfield. Coach Francis had to sponge down Hee Yan's ankle following one crunching collision. Our strikers, Yolanda and Tracey, were starved of the ball. Coach Francis patrolled the touchline, barking instructions and getting red-faced as she did so. To keep warm, I ran on the spot and did the occasional sprint.

The Dames struck our crossbar with a header from their tall centre forward. Her name was Marlene Chivers. Blanka could only watch the ball but when she reclaimed it, she roasted the ears of her defenders. 'Why did you allow the cross into our box. *No friggin' crosses!*'

Our best opportunity came when Maria and Paula did a nice passing move; the ball ended up at Tracey's feet and she hit it first time from the corner of the box. Their keeper appeared in a panic, but she managed to sort out her footwork and tip the ball over the bar.

Coach Francis clapped. 'That's better!' she roared. 'Keep passing, keep moving.'

There weren't any more opportunities for either side before half-time. Coach Francis served orange halves to the players from a plastic bag. I would've preferred something warmer like a hot dumpling and a strip of fried plantain.

'Keep passing the ball,' Coach Francis instructed. 'They're tiring, especially their midfield. Soon they won't be able to press us so hard. Tracey, drop back a bit and play the number-ten role; we need you on the ball a bit more. Get the ball wide when you can, and opportunities will occur. Remember to *concentrate* in defence. That Chivers girl must be close to six foot, so *no crosses*! Close them down early.'

I tried to catch Coach Francis' eye in the hope that she might put me on immediately after half-time. No luck.

The game restarted. Maria enjoyed much more possession. The Dames spent more time taking deep breaths. Hee Yan had less work to do. Tracey was very unlucky with a spin and a shot that hit the goalkeeper's head. There was a pause in play when the referee checked if the goalkeeper was OK. Dionne nearly scored from the resulting corner. We all screamed and protested when Paula was brought down in the penalty area. The referee shook her head and pointed for a goal kick. Tracey wasn't having it. She yelled at the referee, 'Blatant penalty! When's the last time you been to Specsavers? Or did you get lost on the freaking way cos you can't friggin' see!'

Tracey received a yellow card. She yelled a Jamaican swear word that the referee didn't understand. Coach Francis asked Blanka to pull her back so she didn't get herself into any more trouble. I was ordered to warm up.

Oh, my gosh! I'm coming on.

Suddenly I was filled with nervous energy.

Don't mess up, don't mess up, don't mess up.

Three minutes later, I replaced Yolanda. I smiled at her as she trudged off the pitch. She looked a bit pissed.

Coach Francis instructed me to play on the right wing and take on their left full back. I didn't get a touch for five minutes but an exchange of passes with Maria made me feel a bit better.

My second touch was much more positive. I came short to collect a pass from Neesha. I found Maria with my pass and then I sprinted into the right-wing position, making sure I wasn't offside. Maria found me with the perfect ball. I was one-on-one with their defender. She had short chunky legs, and shoulders almost twice the width of mine.

But has she got speed?

I slowed down and approached her with the ball. For a moment I looked up and spotted Tracey and Paula making runs. Suddenly I flicked the ball to my right and a burst of speed took me past the full back. Just before I made it to the touchline, I glanced up, saw Tracey near the penalty spot and pulled the ball back to her. She finished well, aiming the ball at the left corner of the goal. The goalkeeper had no chance.

Goal!

On my first appearance I had made an assist.

Paula, Maria, Neesha and I all jumped on Tracey to celebrate. We fell to the ground, not caring if mud kissed our cheeks. I can't describe the beautiful feeling it gave me. I just closed my eyes and imagined Edson was watching me. *His satisfied smile.* When I got back to my feet, in the distance Blanka performed back flips to mark our first goal. 'Pulverise them!' she roared. 'But don't get complacent.'

We did have a scare with the Chivers girl bulleting a header that slapped our post, but Tracey's cool finish was the only goal.

Everyone smiled as we made our way back to the changing rooms.

'Anyone coming to the Lounge Bar for a drink?' asked Blanka.

'I've got to get home and cook,' said Bernice.

'But you've got a man,' said Dionne. 'Why can't he do it?'

'He can't cook,' explained Tracey. 'The last time he tried, he almost burned the house down.'

'He cremated the rice,' giggled Bernice.

'And the carrots, broccoli and asparagus,' added Dionne.

'That asparagus was damn well expensive!' added Bernice. 'From Waitrose.'

'I'll come,' said Maria. 'The Lounge Bar serves a good red wine. A shame they don't cook paella.'

All right for dem to talk about red wine. Apart from Louella and me, they're all eighteen-plus.

'Do they still do that Caribbean breakfast?' Neesha asked. 'If they do, I'll come.'

'Yes, they do,' replied Blanka. 'Anyone else? Ackee, saltfish, fried plantain, the whole works. Louella? Yolanda? Hee Yan?'

'No alcohol.' Hee Yan shook her head.

'I'm on babysitting duty,' said Yolanda.

'That little monster, Chevron, your nephew?' Paula wondered. 'Who threw his spaghetti Bolognese on the floor the last time you looked after him?'

'Yep,' Yolanda replied. 'I'll be babysitting that same monster. He's all right . . . when he's asleep.'

'And I'm going shopping down Nine Elms Market with my mum,' explained Louella.

'I can't believe it!' Blanka raised her voice. 'We beat the Dames and hardly anyone wants to celebrate. I'll guess I'll have to drink a few beers in your place.'

'We can all celebrate if we win the league,' said Coach Francis. 'We're now three points behind the leaders. If we win, the beers and wines will be on me.'

'What about rum?' Paula wanted to know.

'Hmmmm,' Coach Francis replied. 'Rum's expensive. You

The Girl With the Red Boots

wanna see the price the man sells a flask of Captain Morgan's for at my corner shop.'

'It's what I drink,' smiled Paula. 'White rum, a Diet Coke chaser, a cherry on top and a squeeze of lime.'

Everyone laughed. It was nice to hear all the banter.

'What about you, Kadeen?' Blanka asked. 'I know you're too young to drink, but I can still buy you a soft drink or a mocktail.'

I wondered what a mocktail was. I felt all eyes on me. 'Er . . . no, not today,' I stuttered. 'Me have to get back and . . . help me aunt wid someting.'

Twenty minutes later, I rode the back seat of Coach Francis' car. Once again, I couldn't escape the feline stench. I asked her to drop me outside the Hootananny. Coach Francis climbed out of the car to say goodbye.

'After a nervous start, you did good today, Kadeen. Real good.'

'Thank you,' I replied.

'That's one assist already,' she added. 'And you only played twenty-five minutes. You have pace. You can be a master of tactics and defensive formations but none of that can deal with the raw speed and skill you possess.'

'That's nice of you to say,' I said.

Coach Francis grinned. 'You're my secret weapon. I'll see you at training.'

Louella wound down her window. 'When are you coming to my place?' she asked.

'Soon,' I replied. 'Just got to clear it with my aunt.'

'I'll cook you my lasagne special,' said Louella. 'Don't forget.'

'I won't,' I said, wondering what a lasagne special was.

As Coach Francis pulled away, I felt a surge of goodness. *Secret weapon? I like that.*

18

Ketch Ah Niece

I couldn't kill my joy as I approached home.

I made an assist.

I even forgot the grey clouds and the cold for a few moments.

Glancing ahead, I saw something that chilled my blood more than the English morning frost.

Aunt Mel stood outside our front door. Her arms were folded. Underneath her red headscarf, her glare was hard. She watched my approach like she was a border guard in a war zone. I stared at the ground, hoping she still didn't know about my football excursion.

I climbed the steps slowly. Aunt Mel didn't move apart from one finger that tapped her bicep. She tracked me with her eyes.

'Well?' she said.

'Good afternoon, Aunt Mel. You had a good morning?'

'It coulda been better,' she replied.

I passed her and entered the house. The grip on my rucksack tightened. Guilt stirred in my belly once again. 'How could it be better?' I asked weakly.

'It coulda been better if me never find out that me niece lie to me.'

Me get ketch. Caught in a lie! Oh, Lord!

The jubilation I had following our football victory gushed out of me. Suddenly my head felt warm. My knees wobbled. I heard the front door slam.

I headed to the kitchen and quickly poured myself a glass of water. Aunt Mel followed me in. Sky News was broadcasting silently on the TV. 'Well?' she said.

'Me . . . Me,' I stuttered. 'Me was going to tell you.'

'Then what stopped you?'

'The other night,' I explained. 'You were . . . you were so vex. And you went to your room straight after dinner.'

'That's no excuse, Kadeen!'

'Me . . . me sorry.'

Aunt Mel sat at the dinner table. Her eyes locked on to mine. She pressed her hands together as though she was thinking of an evil punishment. 'You lied to me,' she said. 'Say someting happen to you? Me don't know where you there.'

'Me really sorry,' I repeated.

'I was tidying up your room,' she said. 'Me thought it strange that all of your schoolbooks were on your bedside cabinet.

The Girl With the Red Boots

Especially as you tell me you were going over to Emma's to do a liccle homework. Me already know that you bring your football boots wid you. This morning me could not find dem.'

I sank half of my glass of water. 'But me love football! Me can't just stay inside your yard and stare at the four walls all the while.'

'You have that new friend Emma who you play chess wid,' Aunt Mel argued. 'It's a safe place to go becah she just live up the road. But football? Me don't know the hell where you're going. Who do you play wid?'

'This team,' I replied.

'What team?'

'The SW2s. They're . . . they're a ladies' team. Coach Francis—'

'And who is this Coach Francis?' Aunt Mel cut me off. 'Where did you meet him?'

'Coach Francis is a woman,' I explained. 'She runs and coaches the SW2s. She lives in Tulse Hill.'

Aunt Mel thought about it. I sipped my water again as I waited for her response. At that moment you could've cooked a thick steak on my forehead. I glanced up at the TV. Once again, there was trouble in the Middle East.

'Me can't allow you to play football,' she said. 'Your mother wanted you here to keep you safe but you're lying to me—'

'Me won't lie to you again,' I interrupted. 'Me promise. And . . . and if me can't play football, then Tony Buttons win.'

'What do you mean, Tony Buttons win?'

'He's . . . he's still punishing me. Making me suffer. Yes, him kill Edson and now him stopping me playing a game that me love. Today me made an assist. It was the first time me smile so wide since that bad breed Tony Buttons kill Edson. It felt so good. Like me coming alive again.'

Keeping up her stone-cold glare, Aunt Mel shook her head. I drained my glass and placed it gently on the table. 'But you lie to me!' Aunt Mel raised her voice. 'Me know you going through a hard time. But that's no excuse to lying to me.'

'It won't happen again,' I insisted.

'Oh, no, it won't.'

There was an awkward silence for a few seconds. I stared at the floor. I wanted to take out my phone, but I thought that would be rude. 'So . . . so . . .' I managed. 'Are you going to let me play?'

Aunt Mel stood up. 'No,' she replied. 'Me can't trust you. You'll have to earn that again. Your mother is thousands of miles away in Jamaica and you're my responsibility. If someting happened to you, she'll never forgive me.'

I picked up my glass, washed it in the sink and made my way to my room. I collapsed on to my bed, cursing myself for not telling Aunt Mel about the football thing earlier.

19

Old Harbour News

I gazed at the ceiling for half an hour or so. Then I checked my phone. 2.45 p.m. 7.45 a.m. in Jamaica.

Me shoulda gone for that mocktail wid Blanka.

Sienna should be at home. Maybe she can cheer me up with talk from me hometown. I punched her number.

'Kadeen! Why you don't call me lately?' Sienna replied. 'It'll have to be quick. Me going to church wid mama.'

'But you don't usually go church wid your mum?'

'She want me to go this morning – her friend, Miss Sinclair, sick with diabetes. She want me to pray for her.'

'Oh,' I said. 'Me hope Miss Sinclair gets better quick-time. She the one wid the strange walk and the mash-up toes, right?'

'Yes, that's the one.'

'Me will pray for her too.'

'So? How's tings?' Sienna asked.

I closed my eyes as I prepared to answer. 'Bad, bad, bad,' I said. 'Me Aunt Mel find out that me playing football. A disaster, me tell you.'

'She did? Why you never tell her?'

'Becah she woulda said no for true. She just want me to stay inside her yard and look 'pon the four walls.'

'At least you're safe in England,' Sienna said. 'Me mama hear gunshot when she drive pass Church Pen the other day. She came home that evening cussing pure badword. Too much gun inna Jamaica.'

'Sorry to hear about your mum's experience,' I replied. 'You're right, me safe but cold inna England.'

'It's coming like an everyday ting,' added Sienna. 'All the bad mon have gun. Me don't feel safe.'

'Me have a new friend in South London,' I said. 'Emma her name. She tell me about all the knife crime in the UK. It's not safe anywhere you go.'

'Tings are not too good for Melody right now,' Sienna said. 'Wilson McKenzie want her to stay over at his yard some night.'

'Oh, Lord! She just get kissy-kissy wid him at your beach party. And now him want her to stay over?'

'Yes, Kadeen! Wilson peckish for you know what! Wilson's mama works at the Spanish Town Hospital and sometimes she works the night shift.'

'Didn't Melody say no?' I wanted to know.

'Melody says she's tinking about it. Can you believe it?'

The Girl With the Red Boots

'You need to slap her head back into good sense,' I said.

'Yes, Kadeen,' Sienna agreed. 'But she have the love bug bad, bad, bad. Ever since my party it's been "Wilson this" and "Wilson that". Me know more about Wilson than me own papa! He want Melody to say to her mama that she's staying over wid me! Can you believe that? A liberty!'

'Don't let her do it, Sienna. She need to see reason.'

'Don't worry,' Sienna said. 'Me not going to lie for she. Oh, by the way, me see Cass Buckley yesterday. He asked about you.'

'Him ask about me?' I raised my voice. 'For true? No joke business?'

'No joke business.'

'What did him say?' I wanted to know.

'Him ask how Kadeen is and how she doing.'

'And how did you reply?'

'Me say to him that you're cold like an ice smoothie inna England, but apart from that, you're OK.'

'Did he say anyting else?'

'No,' Sienna replied. 'But him look generally interested in your welfare.'

'Me want to come home,' I said. 'Staying wid Aunt Mel? She nice enough but it too damn cold over here and me can't even play football any more. Me days are long and chilly.'

'Me want you back home too, Kadeen. It's not the same without you. When you reach, maybe you can chat some sense into Melody's head-top.'

I heard another voice. Sienna's mum. 'Sienna! Come off

that blasted phone and put on your shoes. Church time! And this time, make sure you close your eyes when you're praying.'

'Me guess you have to go.'

'Yes,' Sienna said. 'Me will call you later. Try not to fret too much. The days will pass quick, and before you know it we'll be walking along Old Harbour Bay, sinking our toes in the soft sand and catching a liccle sea breeze.'

I closed my eyes and imagined the gentle waves lapping over my feet.

'Me really hope so.'

'Take care, Kadeen.'

'Bye, Sienna. Tell Melody not to do anyting foolish.'

'Me tell her every time. Bye.'

Just as I killed the call, Aunt Mel poked her head round my door and gave me another cold eye-pass. 'By the way,' she said. 'You're grounded until further notice. As soon as you finish school, me want you to come home. Do you hear me, Kadeen?'

'Yes, me hear you . . . but . . . but what about learning chess with Emma?'

Aunt Mel thought about it. 'You can play chess with Emma. But that's all. *Don't* ever lie to me again.'

Me really want to go back home. But say Cass Buckley like me for real. Would he want me to stay over too? Boys that age are too damn peckish.

Aunt Mel sat at the foot of my bed. She thought about something. She dropped her head.

The Girl With the Red Boots

'Are you OK, Aunt Mel?'

'Yes . . . just tinking of the past. When I was a liccle older than you are now.'

'What . . . what happened then?'

Aunt Mel side-eyed me. She clasped her hands together and closed her eyes for a second. 'I was sixteen,' she said. 'He was nineteen.'

'Who was nineteen?' I asked.

She paused and looked around the room. 'His name was Michael. Michael Boxall. He was me first boyfriend.'

Aunt Mel stood up. She gazed at me as if she was deciding to leak something important to her. 'He lived in the Waterhouse district of Kingston. It can get rough down there. Nuff gangs and political violence.'

'Why . . . why are you telling me this?' I asked.

'Becah . . . becah me want you to understand a bit more about me.'

I nodded.

'Michael loved basketball,' Aunt Mel resumed. 'He used to play down at this concrete court near Tivoli Gardens. The good, the bad and the ugly used to watch. Sometimes they would fire dem gun in the air if somebody made a good play. Me watched him play three time. That's all. Me family warn me about stepping down a dangerous part of town.'

'What . . . what happened?'

'That's where he was shot,' Aunt Mel replied. She sat back down. 'Drive-by shooting. A machine gun. Five get killed. The ting was, he really wanted me to watch him play that day.'

'So . . . so sorry to hear.'

I reached out a hand and placed it on Aunt Mel's back. She stared at the wall.

'Me don't talk about this wid anyone,' she said. 'And me won't speak of it again to you . . . Me just wanted you to understand certain tings about me. Why I'm stopping you from playing football. It's not safe out there.'

'I understand,' I said.

Aunt Mel stood up. She gazed at the ceiling for a long moment before leaving.

My insides went a bit funny.

Did that just happen? Poor Aunt Mel. Sixteen? To go through that. Oh, my sweet Lord. Me will pray for her.

20

Louella

Emma came over with her chess set on Tuesday evening. We played very little chess, but we watched a few music videos of Jamaican reggae artists on YouTube. We tried out a couple of new dance moves that cheered me up a little. Emma knew how to move in time to the beat.

'Where you learn that?' I asked.

'YouTube,' Emma replied. 'I just wish I could go somewhere and bust a style. If only we could have outside beach parties like they do in Jamaica.'

'Maybe you could have snow parties?' I joked.

Emma threw a pillow at me.

'Or big-coat-and-scarf parties,' I added.

'At least one day you'll be back home,' Emma said. 'All that sun, sand and music. I'm stuck here with the rain, sleet and cold.'

Louella

'Maybe you could come back wid me,' I said. 'Or visit me the next time you're in Jamaica.'

'That would be something.' Emma smiled. 'Mum's trying to find the money for another trip to Jamaica. If that don't work, I could hide in your suitcase.'

'You miss your dad, don't you?' I asked.

Emma stared out the window for a few seconds before answering. 'Yes, I do. He's got this can-do energy. He's very positive. Sometimes . . . sometimes I hear Mum crying at night. I guess you miss your dad too?'

I thought about Dad driving his pick-up truck. 'Of course. Mum always said he spoiled me too much. But at least me see him regular. Every week or so. He gave me some spending money before me left. Me haven't touched it yet.'

'It's hard to understand,' said Emma. 'Mum hasn't done anything wrong. During the pandemic she was a hero. On our street, they used to clap her all the way to the bus stop on her way to work. Now they won't give the man she fell in love with a full visa. It's all wrong!'

I stood up, went over to Emma and gave her a warm hug.

'At least you get it,' said Emma. 'Some of the teachers at school don't. Even one or two friends say I shouldn't worry about it. And relatives whisper behind my back saying it was just a holiday thing and my mum should look for a partner who's British. I've got this Aunt Veronica who—'

The Girl With the Red Boots

'Kadeen!' Aunt Mel called from the kitchen. 'Kadeen! Dinner ready.'

Emma followed me into the kitchen. Aunt Mel had placed down proper napkins in front of the seating positions – whenever it was just the two of us, we made do with kitchen towel. She had also taken out the fancy glasses from the display cabinet.

The dinner smelled good: slow-cooked gammon, roasted parsnips, carrots and sliced boiled potatoes with an ooze of garlic butter and parsley on top. Aunt Mel had even had time to make her own spicy apple sauce. There was no wine or fruit juices on the table, just a jug of cold water and a bottle of Diet Coke.

'Emma, nice of you to stay for dinner,' Aunt Mel said. 'Me hope you like gammon, and you're not one of these boring people who don't eat pork.'

'I don't mind pork,' replied Emma. 'I love my Cumberland thick sausages that Mum grills on a Friday evening. Thanks.'

I filled everyone's glass with water. As I sank my first mouthful of veg, Aunt Mel turned to me. 'You say that when you played for the SW2s, it made you smile wide for the first time since Edson was taken away from us. Is that true?'

I nodded. 'Me miss Edson every day, but me love me football.'

Aunt Mel thought about something. I glanced at Emma. She had paused eating.

Louella

'Your brother has been taken from you,' Aunt Mel went on. 'I was thinking a lot last night. We're all still grieving him. May he rest in peace. Me don't want to be guilty of taking someting else that you love from you.'

'So . . . so, me can play?'

Aunt Mel wagged a finger at me. 'Not until I meet this Coach . . .'

'Francis,' I added. 'She all right. She's so down to earth that even the worms like her. You will get on wid her. She's like the SW2s' mother. And in the team, there is Louella, Bernice, Blanka and—'

'*Don't* get too excited,' warned Aunt Mel. 'I just want to meet wid Coach Francis. See how she stay. Get to know her for myself.'

'So me can go training tomorrow?'

'Where do you train?'

'At Battersea Park.'

Aunt Mel cut off a generous piece of meat. She stabbed it with her fork and spread apple sauce all over it. She swallowed it before she spoke again. 'And how do you get to Battersea Park?'

'Coach Francis picks me up outside the Hootananny,' I replied.

'From now on, she picks you up outside me front door,' Aunt Mel insisted. 'Do you understand?'

I nodded.

'Will she have time to come in for a liccle talk when training done?'

The Girl With the Red Boots

'Me will ask her.'

'Good, good,' Aunt Mel said. 'Now, eat your dinner.'

'Just . . . just one more ting, Aunt Mel.'

'One more ting? You're not happy wid me giving your football ting consideration?'

'No, no, no,' I replied. 'Me teammate Louella want me to go to her yard for dinner. Me was tinking me could go there before training on Wednesday. Is that all right? She want to cook me this ting called lasagne.'

Aunt Mel ate another mouthful before she replied. 'Where she live?'

'Just five minutes' walk away in Tulse Hill estate.'

'I suppose so.' Aunt Mel side-eyed me. 'But that don't mean you can go uptown, downtown and all over the damn place. You just go to her yard for dinner, go training and come home. Agreed?'

'Agreed.' I smiled.

'Make sure you're polite and thank her very much even if you don't like the lasagne.'

'What is it?' I asked.

'It's cooked mince with a sheet of pasta on top,' Emma said. 'Sometimes they serve it at school. They're not too generous with the mince.'

I looked at Aunt Mel. She didn't seem impressed.

Louella lived on the fifth floor of this brown-brick block named Osgood House. The lift was out of order, so I had to climb the concrete stairs. There were cigarette butts and

Louella

used vapes in the corners. It reminded me of the gulleys back home. Louella lived at flat twenty-seven. It hit me that I never had a white friend in Jamaica.

Where do the white kids in Jamaica go to school? This is going to be different.

The bruised brown door didn't have a doorbell. I slapped the letter box hard and saw a shadow approaching through the misted-wire glass window. The door opened. Louella held a baby of about a year old. It sucked fiercely on a dummy and wore a light-blue onesie.

'Glad you didn't get lost,' said Louella. 'You're right on time for dinner. Meet Timmy, my little brother.'

A bib was tied around Timmy's neck. His cheek was covered with whatever he had been eating. He had fine ginger hair, red cheeks and cute cartoon eyes.

'Hi, Timmy,' I greeted. 'Nice to meet you.'

I stroked his chin. Timmy decided to spit out his dummy, grab my finger and wanted to feed on that.

'He's at that age where he wants to put everything in his mouth.'

I hooked my rucksack on a hallway peg before Louella led the way inside. The walls hadn't been blessed by a lick of paint for many a year. The veneer-like wooden floor tiles were curled in the corners. The smell of cigarette smoke stuck in the air.

We entered the front room. The walls were naked apart from a single wooden cross. Sitting at the small round dinner table were two twin boys. I guessed they were eight years old. They were still wearing their school uniform.

'Meet Liam and Declan,' said Louella. 'Trust me, they're not usually this quiet.'

Holding their knives and forks, they both nodded at me. 'Hi,' I said.

They both chuckled at each other.

'Mum!' Louella called out. 'Mum! Kadeen's here.'

From the kitchen emerged a woman who looked around forty. Maybe forty-five. She had sad blue eyes. Her greying ginger hair was tied up in a ponytail. She had worry lines marking her forehead, and skinny, cracked lips. She wore a green plastic pinafore and tiger-striped slippers. 'Sit down, darling,' she said to me with a welcoming smile.

I pretended not to notice her bad breath.

'Sit down, Kadeen, lovely to meet ya. Louella tells me you come from Jamaica. Miss Delaney, the lady who lives upstairs, comes from there. She's always going on about how she wants to go home for good one day. I'd take a guess that I know more about her hometown, Port Maria, than most of the people who live there. I hope you brought some of that sunshine with ya. We could do with it.'

'It's lovely to meet you too, Miss Elms. Sorry me could not bring any warm sunshine wid me.'

'Just call me Hazel,' Louella's mum said. 'Don't give me any of that formal stuff. It's only the officials at social security who call me Miss.'

Louella passed Timmy to Hazel, who wiped his mouth

Louella

before she sat down with him. 'I have to burp him,' she said.

Two burps later, Louella returned with a hot glass dish of lasagne. It was served with cabbage, mash potato and carrots. It wasn't too bad apart from the rubbery-tasting pasta. I finished it all, reminding myself what Aunt Mel told me. '*Be* polite and nice'.

'Well?' Louella asked. 'What do you think? It's the third time I've cooked it. I've put a bit more pepper in the mince cos Miss Delaney says Jamaican people like their food hot.'

'It's good,' I replied. 'Fills you up. Thanks so much. You'll have to tell me how to make it.'

Louella closed her eyes and breathed out a long sigh of relief. The twins giggled.

'I told you not to worry,' said Hazel. She turned to me. 'She's been fretting about it all last night. She was in a right state, I'm telling ya.'

Following dinner, I excused myself to use the bathroom. There was no proper toilet paper, just a pile of McDonald's serviettes placed on top of the cistern. The thin-tiled flooring was cracked.

Don't judge, I told myself.

When I returned to the table, Timmy was propped between two cushions on a raggedy sofa, Hazel washed the dishes in the kitchen and the twins played in their bedroom. Louella was still at the dinner table checking something on her mobile.

'Since Timmy was born, things have been a bit rough,'

The Girl With the Red Boots

Louella admitted. 'Mum's fighting for more money from the social and trying to get Timmy's dad to cough up a bit more.'

'A bit more?' Hazel repeated from the kitchen. 'He owes me much more than a bit more. He was always a tightarse. I should've known that from the first date. Come to think of it, I should've known that from the second date too.'

'Yep.' Louella nodded. 'Kenny's king of the tightarses. And I'm not talking about his bum.'

'If he won the lottery tomorrow, I'd be lucky to get a packet of peanuts out of him.'

I had to laugh.

When I composed myself, I smiled at Louella. 'So what got you into football?'

'I dunno,' Louella replied. 'I s'pose with Brockwell Park being so close, it was only natural to bring a ball with me one day. I used to play on my own a lot of the time. You know what boys can be like when you ask to join their game.'

'Ah, yes, me know how boys stay,' I said. 'But me brother always wanted to include me. He was different to the rest. He'd take me out to meet all his friends . . .'

Suddenly this wave of grief just filled me, right from my foot-bottom to me head-top. It came out of nowhere. I closed my eyes, but I couldn't stop the tears. All I could see was a smiling Edson playing ball.

'Kadeen? Kadeen? You all right?'

Louella

I wiped my face with my hands and took a couple of deep breaths.

'Sorry,' I said. 'Me don't know what came over me. This is embarrassing.'

'No need to be sorry,' Louella replied. 'And you shouldn't feel embarrassed.'

She came round to where I sat and hugged me. Before she returned to her seat, she kissed me on top of my head. I felt a bit better.

A few minutes later, I told Louella about my loss and made her promise to tell no one.

'Grief is horrible,' she said. 'People think you can get over it in a few days or weeks, but you never really do. You can read all those stupid self-help books but it's always there, you know. Any little thing can stir it up. It can have you crying like a baby who's just had a bee sting.'

I nodded.

'I lost my dad when I was nine,' Louella continued. 'Motorbike accident. A lorry crashed into him as it was turning left. The bike was all twisted and mangled. Mum always said his motorbike would be the death of him. I wouldn't call my mum a prophet, but she was right on that one. He loved football too – Chelsea fan. He supported their ladies' team too. He was a mechanic, always fiddling around with engines. His ambition was to buy a little boat, you know, to take us all out on the sea. His sister lives near Bognor Regis. He wanted to take us for a ride in the sea around there . . . I still miss him.'

'And so do I,' shouted Hazel from the kitchen.

'Sorry . . . sorry to hear,' I managed.

'What about you?' Louella asked. 'What got you into football?'

'Me brother, Edson,' I replied. 'Me earliest memory was him kicking a ball. It's important for me, you know. When we were playing the other day, when me come on as sub, me could forgot all me worries and just play, you know.'

'I know what you mean,' Louella agreed. 'Football gets to you like that. Mum says I swapped one religion for another.'

I glanced at the cross on the wall.

'There's nothing stopping you playing football *and* going to church,' her mum said. 'You just need to find a team that plays on Saturdays.'

'I should give you something to stop listening to my conversations,' snapped Louella.

'I just hope football can make you rich so you can buy me a nice house in Caterham or somewhere,' Hazel laughed. 'Make sure the garden's big enough so I can grow my own spuds, cabbage and tomatoes. I can't believe how much those things cost at the market these days.'

'Caterham!' Louella repeated. 'They'll have to pay me a Premier League's wage for a house there!'

Ten minutes later, someone slapped the letter box.

It was Coach Francis. 'Hi, Louella, Kadeen. Where's Hazel?'

'I'm in here!' shouted Louella's mum.

Louella

Coach Francis and Hazel had a fifteen-minute chat in the kitchen. Before we made our way downstairs to her Mini, Hazel reminded Louella to help her with some social security form she had to fill in.

'Later this evening, Mum,' Louella said. 'Make sure you've got all your paperwork together. I've got so much on. I'm late on homework too.'

We left the flat. As I skipped down the stairs, I wondered if there was a way I could help Louella.

'Me Aunt Mel wants to chat wid you after training,' I said to Coach Francis as I climbed into the back seat.

'Wants to speak with me?' Coach Francis raised her eyebrows. 'She don't want me to talk you out of leaving school too early? Do you remember Clara, Louella? Her ma wanted me to talk her into going to uni. I'm not a social worker. I did the best I could. Wait a minute, you're not pregnant, are you, Kadeen?'

'Lord Jesus cripes! No, no. No. It's nothing like that. Me mother would kill me.'

'Then what's it all about?' Coach Francis asked.

'She . . . she just want to know that me in good hands. You understand.'

Coach Francis grinned before starting the car. 'I've got the safest hands since Pat Jennings retired.'

'Pat who?' I wondered.

Coach Francis pushed into first gear and drove over the road ramps very slowly. 'Well before your time,' she said. 'Pat Jennings had hands the size of the jolly green giant's shovel. He'd pluck the ball out of the air like it was a ping-pong ball.'

I wondered who the hell was the jolly green giant.

Training was tough. We did jogs, sprints and defensive drills. We also spent a lot of time on 'triangles', as Coach Francis called them. In a small-marked square, three players had to pass the ball between each other, and one defender had to hunt for it. If you messed up passing or lost possession, then you had to go in the middle and try to win the ball. When Louella had her turn chasing the ball, I noticed the condition of her boots. They weren't pretty. A seam was torn at the heel, and the leather close to her toes was pulling away from the stud plate.

Everyone had built up a bottle-load of sweat by the time we had finished. I had to admit, I didn't feel the cold. My lungs called for mercy and my calf muscles burned.

When we had changed out of our football kit, Coach Francis stood up from a bench, cleared her throat and watched us. Everyone paid attention apart from me. I studied Louella's boots before she placed them back in her bag.

'When you're quite ready, Kadeen.' Coach Francis side-eyed me.

'Oh, sorry.'

'We're just one point behind the leaders,' she said. 'They drew three-all last Sunday with Stockwell Park Angels. We both have three games to go. Now the title's in our own

Louella

hands. When you go to your bed tonight, I want you to imagine gazing at the little gold cup that they hand out to every player of the title-winning team. And the trophy won't look too bad sitting on my sideboard.'

Edson would be so proud.

'Who are the leaders?' I asked.

'Mitcham Royals,' replied Blanka. 'We play them the last game of the season. And we're going to mash them!'

'We have to keep the pressure up on Mitcham Royals,' Coach Francis continued. 'Let's not have any silly slip-ups before we face them. Let's knock them off their proud perch.'

'They've got an easy run-in,' said Maria. 'Apart from us, they're playing teams near the bottom.'

'And they have to face us at their home ground,' said Coach Francis. 'We've got the Pensioners this coming Sunday. It'll be hard.'

'The Pensioners?' I repeated.

'They're called the Pensioners cos most of their team are over thirty,' explained Louella.

'They foul a lot,' said Yolanda.

'Cos they're too damn slow,' added Tracey.

'And usually the ref lets them get away with it,' said Zoe.

'Whether the ref lets them get away with their fouling or not, we're much the better team,' Coach Francis insisted. 'We'll hit them by moving the ball quickly and using our pace. By the time we finish with them, they'll be making appointments with their doctors complaining of breathing problems. I expect to win at least three-nil. No excuses!'

'Yes!' shouted Blanka. She stood up and clenched her fists. 'Let's crush them like biscuits in a cheesecake, pulverise them! Demolish them!'

'And, Tracey.' Coach Francis pointed at her. '*Don't* allow their aggression to rile you up. Watch your tongue. You got sent off against them last year.'

'I'll try my best,' replied Tracey. 'But they're *cheats*!'

'Even if they are cheats,' Coach Francis said, 'let's play to the ref's whistle. *No* stupid sending-offs.'

Everyone looked at Tracey. Tracey crossed her arms and stared at the floor.

'That's all, girls,' Coach Francis concluded. 'Have a good week. Try and stay off the wine, beer and smokes two days before the game.'

Everyone looked at Neesha.

21

The Long Arm of Tony Buttons

Louella and I returned to Coach Francis' car for the drive home. My heart banged my ribcage. And it wasn't because we had a hard workout. Coach Francis dropped Louella home before turning to me.

'How do I address your Aunt Mel?' Coach Francis asked.

'Just . . . just Aunt Mel is all right.'

Coach Francis followed me into Aunt Mel's house. We found her at the kitchen table enjoying a round bowl of strawberry ice cream and blackcurrant jelly. She sipped a glass of water. Coach Francis went all quiet on me. My stress levels ran up another floor.

Say they don't get on? Aunt Mel might sniff the cat stench from her and think she's weird. She might ground me forever.

'Aunt Mel, this is Coach Francis,' I introduced.

The Girl With the Red Boots

'Sit down, sit down,' said Aunt Mel. 'Do you want some dessert? I thought I would indulge myself. I'm having one of those nights.'

Coach Francis gazed lovingly at Aunt Mel's plate. 'Oh, yes. I've had many of those nights. I can see you're a woman after my own heart! Why not?'

'You, Kadeen?' Aunt Mel offered.

I nodded.

By the time Coach Francis and I had eaten all our dessert, I learned that she had been married three times. Her last husband managed a football team. He had an affair with this crusty German PE teacher called Miss Netzer. When Coach Francis found out, she cut out the crotches from all his boxers, trousers, jeans and tracksuit bottoms and hung them back in the wardrobe. She also scratched a smiley face on the bonnet of his car. Aunt Mel laughed out loud. She decided to bring out the wine. Not just wine. Prosecco. Coach Francis enjoyed a small glass.

This is going well.

'Why do men who are getting it at home want to play away and get it from somewhere else?' Coach Francis wondered. 'He said it wouldn't happen again, but I gave him my orders. I'm not cooking his dinner, scrubbing his skid marks in his boxers and tolerating him seeing some German PE tart who looked like she could crack a walnut between her knees. I'm not having it!'

'Good for you!' Aunt Mel raised a glass. 'Here's to giving the red card to bad men!'

'And to men who can't commit.'

As their conversation continued, I had to bite my lip to stop from laughing.

'I can see Kadeen's in good hands,' said Aunt Mel, walking Coach Francis to the front door. 'I just don't want her to drink any alcohol after games and get up to anyting foolish. She's still a schoolgirl.'

'I'll make sure of that,' assured Coach Francis. 'No alcohol on my watch. Not even a shandy.'

'And the people who attend your games just come for the love of football?' Aunt Mel asked.

'Yes, of course. The crowd mostly consist of friends, boyfriends, girlfriends . . . the odd dog.'

'That's good to hear,' nodded Aunt Mel.

I breathed out a long breath.

Good. Me can play me football. Me might even win a liccle gold cup!

'Why don't you come and watch, Aunty?' I asked.

'Come and watch?' Aunt Mel repeated. 'You expect me to stand up on some frosty touchline inna park on a freezing Sunday morning? No, sah. That's not for me. Maybe if you played in the summer I might watch.'

I followed Coach Francis back to her Mini. 'What do you reckon?' she asked.

'She likes you,' I replied. 'Otherwise she wouldn't have bust out the Prosecco.'

'That's good to know. Your Aunt Mel is quite a character. I'll invite her round to mine one day. I'll cook her a roast with all the trimmings and bake a rhubarb crumble. I hope she doesn't mind cats.'

'I'm not too sure,' I replied. 'I'll ask.'

'OK, Kadeen. I'm looking forward to Sunday's game.'

'Me too,' I said.

When I returned indoors, Aunt Mel had her serious face on. She was speaking to someone on her phone. 'She's here,' she said.

'Who is it?' I wanted to know.

'It's your mother.'

'She OK?' I asked.

'Yes. Speak to her.'

She gave me the phone. We swapped a glance, but she didn't give anything away. 'Hi, Mum. How's tings?'

'Tings are not too bad. How about you? Are you behaving yourself?'

'Of course.'

'Doing good at school? Remember, when you finally reach home, you'll be preparing to sit for your Caribbean Secondary Education Certificate.'

'Yes, me know, Mum.'

I made my way to my room and crashed on to my bed.

'And me OK,' I continued. 'Apart from the cold. It seeps into your bones. I have to keep wriggling my toes to check if they're still there . . . Is there someting you want to tell me, Mum?'

Silence for two seconds.

'Mum?'

The Long Arm of Tony Buttons

'Yes . . . yes, there is,' Mum replied. 'Me not too sure if it's good news or bad news.'

'Why? What's breaking?'

'Me don't want to stress you out.'

'Mum!'

'It's Tony Buttons,' she revealed.

'What about him? If him not dead me not interested.'

'They found him. He's in police custody.'

'Yes!' I shouted. 'They should hook him up on a sharp wire over a bridge and let people fling rockstone after him. Or they could suspend him from a helicopter and dip him inna the sea where the broad sharks roam. That brute! Me hope he gets two hundred years inna jailhouse. No, no, no, jailhouse is too good for him. They should—'

'Kadeen, calm down.'

'Calm down? That's the goat shit who killed me brother! They should string him up by his seed bags!'

'Kadeen!'

'Sorry, Mum.'

I took a few breaths.

'They're extraditing him back to Jamaica,' Mum explained. 'It'll take a liccle time. And he will need to be identified by witnesses following what happened to Edson.'

Witnesses. For a short moment, I couldn't speak.

'He was trying to catch a flight from Fort Lauderdale to Toronto,' Mum revealed, 'using a false passport.'

'What . . . what do you mean, he will need to be identified?' I wanted to know.

The Girl With the Red Boots

I heard Mum suck in a breath.

'When they finally return him to Jamaica, the police want you and a few other witnesses to identify that he was the man who was escaping in the white pick-up truck.'

'Oh, Lord Jesus cripes,' I said. 'Me have to be in the same room as him?'

'No,' Mum replied. 'Not necessarily. You will see him, but he won't be able to see you. You're a minor. I'll be with you, and Officer Crystal Myers. It will take place at a different police station – not Old Harbour.'

'When?' I asked.

'Dem tell me a few weeks or so, when they finish all the bureaucracy,' Mum said. 'The Belize authorities want to arrest him too. We still have to keep you safe. The Florida police have already checked his phone. He has contacts in New York, LA, Belize, Colombia, Toronto and London.'

'London!' I repeated. 'They might track me down.'

'Relax, Kadeen. Him don't know what you look like.'

'How do you know?'

'Highly unlikely. Try not to tink about it too much. Just get on wid your life in England.'

'Get on wid me life? When me know that brute Tony Buttons has him gangster bredren in London too. Me might as well come back home now.'

'No, no, Kadeen. The police want you to stay where you are until the right time. He has more friends in Jamaica than anywhere else. You're important for the prosecution. They want to build up a strong case.'

The Long Arm of Tony Buttons

'Me couldn't be the only person who sight Tony Buttons making him getaway.'

Another silence. This time for five seconds.

'Mum?'

'The police believe that they can get two more people to testify seeing Tony Buttons driving away that day.'

'Just two? Are you serious? Downtown Old Harbour was ram that day. Nuff people about.'

'They're doing all they can to make the case against him tight like surgical glove. Me want to see that man . . . No, he's not a man. Me want to see that *devil* pay for what him do to Edson. Don't you want the same ting, Kadeen?'

'Yes, of course, Mum.'

'Good,' she said. 'Man like that shouldn't see another blessed dawn. Me hope God rots his body inna cell for the rest of his days.'

'Me glad they ketch him,' I said.

'But be careful, Kadeen,' Mum warned. 'Don't do *anyting* to bring attention to yourself.'

'I won't.'

'Oh, by the way.'

'What is it, Mum?'

'Me hear about your football excursions. Aunt Mel tell me.'

'But, but, but what me suppose to do while me here inna England? Look 'pon the four walls and get bored outta me mind? Me can't just do school, homework, school, homework. Me used to being outside doing someting.'

The Girl With the Red Boots

'Just be careful, Kadeen,' Mum said. 'Keep your personal business to yourself. You never know who might be listening or chatting behind your back.'

'Me will be careful, Mum.'

'One last ting, Kadeen. *Don't* lie again to your Aunt Mel. She don't like that kinda ting. You understand?'

'Me understand.'

'And it's good that she told you about what happened to her first boyfriend.'

'Good?' I repeated.

'Yes, very good,' Mum said. 'It means she trusts you. For months, Mel could not even talk about it. Not even to our parents. Even now, she don't like to discuss it wid me. It's very deep.'

'Oh,' I replied. 'It's a terrible ting. Gunmen mash up so many people's life.'

'They sure do.'

I went to my bed that night not only reliving that dreadful day when Edson was shot dead and worrying about identifying Tony Buttons, but also dreaming of holding a little gold cup in my hands. *It'll be a nice ting to show off to Sienna, Melody and Cass Buckley when I finally reach home.*

22

Flipping and Flopping

'Did you enjoy it, Kadeen?'

We had just bounced an hour's session at Floppy-Flips, this trampoline place in Balham, South London. Emma wanted to treat me and cheer me up. She said I'd been miserable since after Wednesday.

'Me don't know,' I finally replied. 'It's like part of me insides are still flipping and flopping. Me don't tink me brain settle yet. What day is it?'

'It's Friday. School over for the week.'

'And me still here in South London? Sometimes me get so high me tink me bounce into North London.

Emma laughed. She had this high-pitched chuckle that creased up her cheeks.

'All me can say it was an experience,' I continued. 'Me never realise you could reach so far.'

The Girl With the Red Boots

'I didn't know it was your first time on a trampoline,' Emma said.

'Me should've said. They don't have these kinda tings back inna Jamaica. Not inna Old Harbour anyway.'

'You still worried about this Tony Buttons G?'

I looked out of the window of the double-decker bus and drummed my fingers against the seat in front of me. The grey clouds were darkening.

'Yes,' I admitted. 'Someone could *come out at any time* and do me . . . someting.'

'Try not to think like that, Kadeen. Look how big London is. I think it's seven or eight million people live here. This Tony Buttons is in custody. He and his bredren have no idea what you look like.'

'But they knew where we lived,' I replied. 'And if they knew where we lived, they know my name. Edson's murder was reported in the newspaper back home. Remember the corrupt police officer at Old Harbour Police Station me tell you about? Clive Hibbert. Traitors are all about.'

'But they don't know where you are now,' Emma reassured. 'Come on, think positive. It's Friday. When we get off the bus, I'll buy you a KFC.'

'Me not too sure if me could keep it down.'

'Come on, Kadeen! Don't make sadness take over you. And I'll watch you play on Sunday. I promise.'

'You will?'

'Of course I will. Even though it's a mad time I have to get up in the morning.'

Flipping and Flopping

I felt good inside. I managed a smile.

'Me hope it don't snow,' I said. 'Oh, Emma, come wid me tomorrow to the sports store. There's someting me have to buy.'

'Like what?'

'It's for a friend. You'll see.'

Twenty minutes later, we jumped off the bus on Brixton Hill.

The traffic was just as bad as it gets in Kingston Town. The only difference was drivers didn't toot their horns so much in London. And everyone walked so much quicker here. I guess they wanted to get in from the cold.

'You'll be all right?' Emma asked.

'Me tink so,' I replied. 'It's just that every time me close me eye, me see that devil pickney Tony Buttons.'

'Maybe,' Emma said, 'maybe you need to see a counsellor or somebody. I think you've got post-traumatic stress or something.'

'Post-traumatic what? No, me just missing Jamaica . . . and my mum, my dad, my friends . . . Edson. Me never tell him how much of a good brother he was to me.'

'Don't be shy, Kadeen. These counsellor people can help.'

'Hmmm? Me not too sure about sharing me personal business to strangers. But you will definitely come on Sunday? Coach Francis picking me up at nine a.m. sharp.'

'Nine a.m.,' Emma replied. 'That's crazy early. I'll have to get up at eight. My mum will wonder what's happened to me if she sees me at that time on a Sunday morning. I'll usually lay in till about eleven.'

'Eleven?' I repeated. 'What do you do in that time?'

'Sit down with my quilt over my shoulders, watching something on Netflix or listening to music.'

'My mum would never let me lie in till eleven,' I said. 'House have to clean, back yard has to be trimmed, you know, chores, chores and more chores.'

Emma's face creased up again.

'Edson only had to take out the rubbish . . .'

Grief licked me again. It was like a punch I never saw coming. Emma put an arm around my shoulders. She didn't have to say anything.

23

SW2s v Pensioners

Coach Francis tooted her horn at 8.54 a.m. The weather app on my phone told me it was three degrees outside. I turned to Emma, who had just sunk a mug of hot chocolate. Her fingers were red. When she arrived ten minutes ago she had looked like a ghost. 'You ready?' I asked.

'I'm not sure if I wanna step outside again,' she said. 'God knows how you play football in this cold.'

Emma wore one of them Russian fur hat things, a huge puffy jacket and a pair of fur-lined boots. I led her outside. She sniffed something as we climbed into the back of Coach Francis' car.

'This is me good friend Emma,' I introduced. 'She don't usually like football but she want to watch me play.'

'Welcome, Emma,' Coach Francis said. 'Welcome, welcome. We need all the support we can get.'

The Girl With the Red Boots

'And, Louella, this is for you.'

From my holdall I pulled out a black box with three yellow stripes running across it. I presented it to Louella. Her eyes went a bit funny. She looked at me, glanced at Coach Francis and gazed at me again. She opened the box and took out one brand-new football boot. She checked the texture of the leather and ran her fingers over the studs and the stitching. She spoke softly. 'Kadeen . . . Kadeen . . .'

'Me . . . me noticed the pair you were wearing were kinda tired, you know. Coming to the end of their days.'

Louella slowly shook her head. One of her eyes became watery. A lone tear dropped on to her left cheek. Coach Francis paused from starting the car as a smile grew from her lips.

'Why . . .?' Louella managed. 'How?'

'Why not?' I replied. 'Before me left Jamaica, me dad give me a liccle spending money.'

Louella clicked off her seatbelt, turned round and gave me a long hug. 'Thank you,' she whispered into my ear. 'Thank you. I'd better play bloody good today.'

'Yes.' I nodded. 'You better play damn good.'

'Can we get the dramatics over,' said Coach Francis. She mopped away a tear. 'We don't wanna be late. What kinda example will that set? Louella, put your seatbelt back on.'

I felt a glow inside.

It's good to give. Me hope Dad doesn't mind what me

SW2s v Pensioners

did wid the money he gave me. Me did buy shin pads for meself.

When we arrived at the playing fields, Coach Francis told me that I'd be a substitute. I stared at the ground and placed my hands on my hips. I spotted a stray football. I wanted to kick it in the air as high as I could and make it land on Coach Francis' head.

There was a touch of frost on the grass and the pitch sloped from one goal to the other. Both penalty areas had brown bare patches. There were about fifty spectators including Emma and me. I guessed most of them were boyfriends and girlfriends. Maybe the odd parent too.

'Bernice and Dionne,' Emma said, watching my teammates warm up. 'Tall, aren't they.'

'Yes.' I nodded. 'They're our central defenders.'

'And Maria's so short.'

'She's the best passer in our team.'

'And where is Hee Yan from?'

'South Korea,' I replied. 'She's a student. She has nuff energy.'

I couldn't understand why I wasn't playing, especially as Coach Francis had said she wanted to use speed against the Pensioners.

'Sorry,' I said to Emma on the touchline. 'Hopefully I'll get on in the second half.'

'Don't worry about it,' she said. 'But don't forget you're still coming to watch me play chess against this other school this coming Thursday.'

The Girl With the Red Boots

'Of course.'

The game started. Every few minutes I jogged along the touchline to keep myself warm. Aunt Mel had bought me a pair of black leather gloves and I thanked the Lord for that.

We played uphill in the first half and enjoyed most of the ball, but we couldn't find the breakthrough. 'Go wide, go wide!' hollered Coach Francis from the touchline. 'Use the space! Create a one-on-one opportunity.'

Maria did as she was told. She released Tracey down the right wing. The Pensioners' left back pulled back her shirt. Free kick. Tracey threw up her arms. 'Ref! Ref! Aren't you gonna book her for that? That's twice now!'

'Play on,' said the ref. 'You've got your free kick.'

'She pulled my shirt!' Tracey ranted.

'And I've given a free kick,' replied the referee. 'Play on!'

Bernice, Dionne and Louella went forward to try and get on the end of a cross. They couldn't make a connection. Their goalkeeper caught the ball confidently. Tracey again complained about something to the referee.

'Watch your language,' warned the official.

Coach Francis put her forefinger against her lips. Tracey ignored her.

Five minutes later, Neesha split the Pensioners' defence with a perfect pass. Tracey was in the clear. She zoomed towards the goal. Boof! This time the centre back hacked her down from behind.

Isn't that a sending-off offence?

Instead, the referee booked the defender. Meanwhile, Tracey took off her left boot, rolled down her sock and furiously rubbed the back of her ankle. She got up and ran towards the offender with serious intent.

Oh, my gosh. Is she going to tump the woman down? This could get ugly.

Maria rushed to intervene with the help of Yolanda, Hee Yan, Blanka and Neesha. They managed to hold Tracey back.

That was a close one.

Tracey was booked for abusive language. Coach Francis shook her head. 'She's gonna blow a gasket,' she said under her breath. There was a whole heap of pushing and shoving. I learned some new English swear words on this day.

'They're effing cheats!' Tracey screamed. 'Effing cheats!'

'Interesting language,' joked Emma. 'We don't get that at chess club.'

Coach Francis turned to me. 'Kadeen, warm up.'

'Now?' I replied.

'Yes, now. I'm putting you on.'

'For real?'

'Yes, for real. Get a move on.'

Coach Francis waved her arms at the referee at the next break in play. She pointed at Tracey. 'Substitution!'

Oh, my gosh! I'm coming on. Hope Tracey doesn't get too vex. By the way she's looking, she might box me down.

'Take Tracey's position,' Coach Francis instructed. 'Their

The Girl With the Red Boots

centre back and left back have already been booked. Your pace will give them another nightmare. If there's gonna be any sending-offs, let it be from their team.'

I ran on to the pitch. I offered my hand to Tracey. She didn't accept it. Instead, she stared at the ground, cursing badwords.

Me better play damn good!

I was caught offside with my first run. I clumsily controlled my second touch and lost possession. Nerves and adrenaline messed up the vibes in my legs. Coach Francis clapped her hands and pointed to her head. 'Concentrate!'

Tracey brewed and steamed beside her.

Me better not mess up.

'Come on, Kadeen!' Emma shouted.

Me can do this. Edson believed in me. Imagine you're back home, dribbling with the ball on the way home from school.

Two minutes later, Neesha won the ball in midfield. She looked up. I made my run. I was onside. She found me with a perfect pass. The defenders weren't quick enough to even foul me. I was five metres clear. The goalkeeper ran out to try and block my shot. I dribbled around her, just like I tricked my way around stones, cones and my schoolmates back home in Old Harbour. The goal was empty. I kicked the ball towards it. The bottom of the net bulged.

Goal!

Yolanda was the first to jump on my shoulders. Blanka

sprinted from her penalty area and almost knocked me out when she joined the celebrations. When I finally got back to my feet, the rest of my team high-fived me. I was a bit dazed, but I didn't care.

Coach Francis was going frantic on the touchline. Her arms were pointing this way and that. 'Concentrate!' she yelled. 'Focus! Back to your defensive positions. Kadeen! Don't get too cocky.'

I didn't know what cocky meant. I guess she meant don't get too boasty.

The Pensioners could no longer play for a draw. They took chances that offered us opportunities. On one counter-attack, Paula hit the bar with a fierce shot. The goalkeeper must've got a fingertip to it cos the referee pointed for a corner. I decided to stand just outside the penalty area. Heading the ball wasn't my thing. Our tall girls, Bernice, Dionne and Louella, crowded near the goal.

Maria curled in the corner. Dionne managed to get a head to it. The ball was cleared off the goal-line. It ricocheted off a defender's knee and bounced out to me. I didn't think. Only one thing was on my mind.

Shoot.

As one of their midfielders rushed out towards me, I caught the ball sweetly on the half-volley. The ball flew towards the top of the net.

Goal! Two-nil!

I couldn't believe it. A pleasure overload rushed through my head. I spread out my arms and went on this mad run. I swerved to my left and then to my right. I thought about doing a somersault but decided not to. I'd look like a damn fool if it went wrong. Louella was the first to catch me. Blanka was the next. Before I knew it, all my teammates were on top of me. I heard the applause from the touchline. Even Tracey clapped. I ran back inside my half and glanced at Coach Francis.

'*Don't* get cocky,' she called out. 'We haven't won the game yet. Concentrate.'

It seemed like I had a superpower in my feet and legs. I didn't feel the cold, nor the tough tackles. I just experienced these dreamy few moments where I felt I wasn't running, but floating.

'*Kadeen!*' Coach Francis screamed. '*Kadeen!* Stop admiring yourself and think about what you're doing.'

The referee blew the half-time whistle. Emma jumped up and down before giving me a hug. 'You're soooo good,' she said. 'Didn't realise how good. That second goal! Wow! Lucky nobody got in the way. It would've taken their head off.'

'Let's have you in a huddle,' Coach Francis said. 'Come on. Quickly.'

We formed a small circle. As I joined in, we all fist-bumped each other. I really felt part of the team. Emma shared out the halved oranges.

'Keep using the space out wide,' Coach Francis instructed. 'I can see three or more goals for us in the second half. Keep working when we haven't got the ball.

SW2s v Pensioners

Harass their right back; she's not so confident on the ball. We can push up a bit, defend higher up. They haven't got any pace in their attack.'

The Pensioners decided to defend at all costs for the rest of the game. Maybe they didn't want to be embarrassed by a high score. We had chances but we wasted them. Paula and Maria struck the woodwork with good shots. I was breathing hard near the end of the game. My legs began to ache.

Me need to work on me stamina.

Louella broke up a rare Pensioners attack. She passed the ball to Maria. Maria found me in the centre circle. Yolanda made a run. She raised her left arm and screamed for the ball. 'Kadeen! Over here!'

Not too hard, not too hard.

I played the ball into Yolanda's stride. She controlled it well. She was one-on-one with the goalkeeper. She went around her and then kaboosh! The goalkeeper brought her down.

Penalty!

The referee pointed to the spot. The Pensioners made no complaint. Yolanda picked up the ball and threw it over to Maria, who held it for a while. She then turned to the referee. 'How much time left?' she asked.

'Three minutes.'

Maria thought about something and then lobbed the ball over to me. 'Go and get your hat-trick.' She smiled. '*Buena suerte.*'

The Girl With the Red Boots

'Thanks,' I said.

Oh, my gosh, she's given me the ball. Me can't miss this.

I placed the ball on the spot. I took in three deep breaths before I stepped five paces back. I wanted to place the ball in the left corner. Hands on hips, I glanced at the goalkeeper. I felt the eyes of Emma, Tracey, Coach Francis and the rest of my teammates burning into me. Edson too. This one was for him. I inhaled through my nose and exhaled through my mouth, a relaxing trick he taught me.

Never rush a penalty, he'd said. *Make the goalkeeper wait for you.*

I ran up to the ball. I made a sweet connection. The goalkeeper dived the wrong way.

Goal! Oh, my Lord, me scored a hat-trick!

This time I simply stood on the spot looking up at the sky. I imagined Edson watching me through the bit of blue that was up there. I think it was Blanka who almost knocked me over with a bear hug. Louella kissed me on the forehead, and Maria walked up to me smiling. '*Felicidades!*'

I guess she congratulated me in Spanish.

'*Chukahamnida!*' said Hee Yan, slapping me on my back.

I couldn't remember what happened during the rest of the game. I was just drifting on this pleasure overload. I couldn't wait until I told my dad, my mum, Aunt Mel, Sienna and Melody.

Me scored a hat-trick! Me wonder if anyone filmed it with their phone or tablet? That would be a cool ting to share.

SW2s v Pensioners

When the referee blew for full-time, the first person on the pitch was Tracey. She jogged towards me and embraced me. 'That was the bees' honey,' she said. 'So much composure. I've got a fight on my hands to keep my place.'

'Thank you,' I said. 'Me said to meself that me better play damn good if Coach Francis put me on so early.'

'Let me tell you, you played pretty damn good. We're gonna win the league this year. I can just feel it. A liccle gold cup would bless my mantelpiece in my front room.'

'You've never won it?'

'No, it's always Mitcham Royals. They've won it for the last three seasons.'

'We'd better put a stop to that,' I said. 'It can't go so.'

'No, it can't go so.'

When we returned to the changing rooms, Blanka stood on a bench and started a song.

'They can't get close to the teen on our team. One of the quickest we've ever seen, yes, our Queen Kadeen on the wing!'

The team liked the lyrics, so they repeated it. The insides of my belly went all wobbly.

'THEY CAN'T GET CLOSE TO THE TEEN ON OUR TEAM. ONE OF THE QUICKEST WE'VE EVER SEEN, YES, OUR QUEEN KADEEN ON THE WING!'

Everyone clapped afterwards, even Tracey.

Gosh, if only Edson could hear that.

Fifteen minutes later, Coach Francis drove us back to Brixton Hill. If I'd tried to fly home, I'm sure I would've managed it.

'The ball!' I shouted. 'Shouldn't me have collected the ball? Me scored a hat-trick.'

Coach Francis laughed. 'This is not the Premiership,' she said. 'Balls cost money. We can't be giving them away every time someone scores a hat-trick. Don't worry, Kadeen, in my match report to the league secretary, I'll big you up.'

'I took some pics,' added Emma. 'Especially after you scored the penalty, and you stood there like a queen. Yeah, that was a nice one.'

'Forward them all to me and I'll send them to my family and friends in Jamaica. Thanks so much.'

'On Wednesday I'm gonna have to bring you down to earth,' Coach Francis said. 'When players get cocky, they lose focus. Until then, celebrate your hat-trick. It was a fantastic performance from someone so young. You've earned your doughnuts today.'

'Thank you,' I said.

We dropped Emma off first. She said she'd see me at school and to remember her inter-school chess tournament on Thursday.

'Of course,' I said. 'Me will be there chanting from the sidelines.'

Coach Francis pulled up outside my place next. Louella jumped out to walk me to my door. 'Thanks again for the boots,' she said. 'I played all right in them today. Kept their winger quiet. My old ones were falling apart. To be honest, it started to get embarrassing playing in them.'

'No need to be embarrassed,' I said. 'Some kids back home play in their bare feet.'

'Before you leave,' she said, 'I'm gonna get you something. Or give you a treat. I don't know what yet, but I will.'

'You don't have to.'

'You didn't have to either, but you did,' Louella said. 'Enjoy the rest of your Sunday.'

'Say hi to your mum, the twins and Timmy for me.'

'I will.'

24

Dulwich College

Thursday rolled around really quickly.

As I stepped off the minibus, I took in my surroundings. 'Is . . . is this a school?'

'Yep,' replied Emma. 'Dulwich College. Your parents gotta have a sack of money to come here.'

The main school building looked like a cross between a palace and a cathedral. The sports grounds were the biggest I had ever seen. There were rugby pitches, football pitches and what looked like a green to play cricket on.

'Oh, yes, Louella said. How much money?' I asked.

'Grands and grands,' said Emma.

Miss Sharna Jackson, who taught physics and managed the school chess team, led us inside. She wore a smart sky-blue-coloured trouser suit and stacked white trainers.

Gosh, this place is full of long corridors with polished wooden floors and paintings of old people hung up on high walls. Everyting is so quiet and ordered.

We passed Dulwich College students wearing perfectly fitted black blazers and blue-and-red-striped ties. 'Good afternoon,' they said.

Gosh, they're proper polite.

'Let's behave ourselves while we're here, shall we,' Miss Jackson said. 'We don't want them to think we're beneath them in any way. Keep your voice down when you have finished your match and remember to shake hands with your opponent whatever the result.'

We followed Miss Jackson up a flight of stairs. I felt intimidated by the photographs of old men who stared at me from the walls.'Emma, Emma. How does this tournament work?'

'Seven of us play seven of them,' she explained.'We get two points for a victory. One point for a draw. No points if you lose. The league has ten schools in it. We're in fourth place. Last year we came eighth.'

'That's not too grubby,' I said.

We were led into a library that was named after this old-school writer, Raymond Chandler.

'Any of his books any good?' I asked.'Was he American?'

'No idea,' Emma replied.

'He was one of the best crime writers this country has ever produced,' said Miss Jackson.

She must've been listening.

'And he was *not* fully American,' Miss Jackson added.

'He arrived in London at just twelve years old. His important education was here.'

There were seven tables with chessboards neatly placed on them. The varnished chess pieces were carved out of dark wood and a lighter-coloured wood – maybe pine. Green leather chairs awaited the players. I felt nervous for Emma.

Refreshments blessed a long table. Sandwiches, mini sausage rolls, chocolate finger biscuits, shortbread, Victoria sponge cupcakes, chocolate rolls, apples, bananas, orange and apple juice and a large jug of icy water.

I licked my lips.

Coach Francis don't serve this kinda ting at half-time.

'Emma, Emma,' I called.

'Yeah.'

'Me have one question,' I said. 'Do we eat before the matches start or after?'

'Before,' she said. 'We spend fifteen minutes or so getting to know each other.'

I served myself a cheese and Branston pickle sandwich and a couple of chocolate mini rolls before the matches began. No, tell a lie. I had three of those. I got chatting to this Dulwich College student called Morris. He guessed correctly that I was from Jamaica.

'Noël Coward owned a property on the north coast,' he said. 'It was called Firefly. I found that out when my parents rented a villa that overlooked the sea near Port Maria. We went to James Bond Beach on that holiday.'

'Who's Noël Coward?' I asked.

'The English playwright.'

'Last year me walk by Beenie Man's house,' I said. 'Me sooooo wanted to knock 'pon him door. Me dad installed solar panelling in a house on the same street.'

'Beenie who?' Morris wondered.

'Beenie Man,' I replied. 'The *king* of the dancehall. The girls dem sugar!'

'Time!' someone shouted.

It all went quiet. The players went to their seats.

The tournament began.

Miss Jackson moved from table to table, giving nods of encouragement. I found a chair and watched Emma's game. Both players had the mark of deep concentration on their foreheads. Spectators whispered here and there. About twenty moves in, Emma took her opponent's queen. I couldn't resist it. 'Yes!' I called out. 'Forward, Emma! Now go for the jugular! Kill his king!'

Everyone looked at me. Miss Jackson's eyes might have well been lasers. She didn't say anything, but I felt the intensity of her glare.

'Sor . . . sorry,' I managed.

Ten minutes later Emma's rival, a long-haired boy with untold badges on his blazer, tipped his king over. He conceded. I wanted to holler out again but this time I stopped myself. *Two points!*

Emma half smiled, stood up and shook hands. I gave Emma a hug. 'You twist up him brain, put an extra line 'pon him forehead and mash him up,' I said. 'Congrats!'

The Girl With the Red Boots

'Shush,' said Emma, glancing over her shoulder at Miss Jackson.

Emma celebrated with two sausage rolls and an orange juice. I sank another chocolate mini roll. They were just too damn delishi-ocious. My phone vibrated. I picked it up and didn't answer. It was Louella. *Can't chat now.*

We followed Miss Jackson around the library. The score was 3-3. Tension filled the room. Last game to finish was our player, Nuno Figo, a Year 8 boy from Portugal, against this Dulwich College student Nigel Coleman. He had even more badges than Emma's challenger.

Where did he find the time to do archery?

'Nuno only started at the school seven months ago,' Emma whispered. 'He didn't speak too much English.'

Not many pieces were left on the board. Both queens were taken. Nuno was under pressure. Emma explained to me that if Nuno survived the next five minutes, the match would be declared a draw. He defended his king like a ghetto boy defending a hot KFC wing. Nigel Coleman shook his head like he didn't know what to do. Stalemate!

We celebrated the draw like it was a victory.

'Yes!' I blurted out. 'Nuno! You're massive! Big up all the chess players inna Portugal!'

Miss Jackson didn't seem to mind my hollering this time around.

'They've beaten us every time we've come here,' said Emma. 'First time we've got a draw.'

Miss Jackson went round hugging every member of the

team. At one point I thought she was going to burst into tears. The smile on her face grew wide again as she shook hands with the Dulwich College chess-team manager. By his expression, the sting of a draw licked him hard, or he had just sunk a sausage roll that didn't agree with him. 'Well played.' Miss Jackson grinned. 'Well played. No one deserved to lose.'

Miss Jackson did a little dance when she thought no one was looking.

My phone rumbled. It was Louella once again. She sent a message.

Can't you talk?

Not at the moment. With Emma at her chess match. I'll call you back when me reach home.

Make sure you do, it's important.

OK.

Me wonder what that's all about?

25

Hot Profile

Before we set off home, Miss Jackson decided to give a speech on the minibus. 'When our chess club was first established, I had to fight for funds to buy the chess sets. Now look at you all. You went pawn to pawn with Dulwich College, the league leaders, and you're going home with a draw. A massive achievement. Tell your parents, tell your friends. Feel very proud.'

I grabbed hold of Emma's arm. 'Feel very proud,' I repeated.

Miss Jackson side-eyed me before she continued. 'Also, top marks on your behaviour. You represented the school very well today. I'll be asking the headmaster if he can mention your performance in the next school assembly.'

Emma's eyes had gone all watery. I guess her winning

her chess match today gave her the same feeling as me scoring a hat-trick.

We were dropped off at school and made our way home from there.

'That's someting to tell your dad next time you talk to him,' I said.

'Oh, yes.' Emma nodded. 'I just wish . . .'

I knew how she felt. We linked arms for the rest of the walk home. I decided to follow her to her front door.

'Thanks for watching me play,' Emma said. 'First thing I'm gonna do when I finish my dinner is call my pops.'

'Yes, you do that,' I said. 'Have a great evening.'

I thought about my own dad.

Me better call him this evening.

I took out my phone. I had received two more messages from Louella. I decided to call her. 'Louella.'

'Kadeen!'

'What's going on? You OK?'

'Yes, I'm good. Guess what? You're in the local newspaper and on their website.'

'What? The newspaper! How?'

'The report of our game,' Louella explained. 'Let me read it to you . . ."SW2s' new signing, fourteen-year-old Kadeen Best, blitzes the Pensioners with a twenty-minute hat-trick. She slotted home her first goal after she sprinted clear of the Pensioners' defence, her second was a thunderbolt from just outside the penalty area and her third was a coolly taken penalty. A new star has arrived in the South London Women's League."'

'And . . . and it's in the newspaper for true? And online?'

'That's what I'm trying to say. In black and white in the *South London Press*. You're famous, Kadeen!'

'How big is this newspaper?' I asked.

'What do you mean?' Louella replied.

'How many people read it?'

'Er, not too sure, but it's on sale in every newsagent in South London. More people read it online. If you want, I'll cut it out for you and photocopy it.'

'How did it get in the newspaper?'

'Every week the managers or coaches file a report of their game to the league secretary. The league secretary picks one or two match reports and sends them on to the newspaper. I think they're one of the league's sponsors.'

'Oh, me see.'

'I thought you'd be more excited, Kadeen. You know what this means?'

'Er . . . no.'

'It means that scouts from professional clubs might come to our next game.'

'Seriously? From Chelsea, Arsenal or Manchester City? Or even Barcelona?'

'Er . . . maybe not Barcelona.'

'You never know.'

For a short second, Louella had killed my joy. 'But it's still a big ting, right?'

Hot Profile

'That's what I'm saying, Kadeen!' Louella agreed. 'It's a massive biggie. Only Tracey has got in the papers before. Nearly two years ago when she scored a hat-trick when we won a thriller six-five. But she was eighteen. You're just fourteen! Sky News should be broadcasting that from their towers! Alex Scott should be interviewing you for *Football Focus.*'

Silence. I could only think of Mum's warning.

You never know who might be listening or chatting behind your back.

Tony Buttons grew large in my head. He was in 3D. A gun was in his hand. He aimed it at me. His finger was about to pull the trigger. *Bang!* A ripple of blood.

'Kadeen . . . Kadeen? You all right?'

'Yes, me good. Me . . . me just can't believe it. Take a pic of the article and send it over to me. Thanks.'

'Of course.'

'Have a good evening.'

'And you too.'

Moments later, she pinged over a WhatsApp message. There it was. A small article about our game last Sunday close to the back page. They had written Kadeen with a giant K. My grin was broader than Kingston harbour. I wanted to sing to the heavens.

Kadeen Best scored a hat-trick! Edson would be smiling. I heard his voice in my head. *You see, sis. You can make it as a baller. Believe!*

I forwarded the article to Sienna and Melody. Before I

reached home, Sienna had sent a reply full of smiley faces and fireworks.

Don't forget me when you're rich and famous, texted Melody.

'Aunt Mel! Aunt Mel!'

'Me in the kitchen, Kadeen.'

I couldn't delete the joy on my face. Aunt Mel sipped a Jamaican soup she had cooked a couple of days ago. I could see the pieces of yam, green banana, mutton and dumplings in her bowl. Steam rose from her meal. It smelled very good. I sat down opposite her. She looked up. Her tired eyes told me she'd had a long day at work.

'What sweet you?' she asked.

I passed her my phone.

'Oh, my goodness!' she said. 'Is this the *South London Press*?'

'Yes.' I nodded. 'Can you believe it?'

'This . . . this is fantastic. Me can't remember anybody of our family being in the newspaper for sports before. Me have to buy a copy and send it to your mother.'

'Me was tinking the same ting.'

'Let me warm up your dinner, Kadeen. We could do wid some good news.'

She used a ladle to pour my soup into a bowl. Reality must have smacked her hard before the microwave did its thing. Her eyebrows had angled and there was another worry line in her forehead when she served my dinner.

'Let's . . . let's hope that certain bad people don't read this, and good people do.'

'Yes . . . let's hope.'

'Don't let it spoil your achievement, Kadeen,' Aunt Mel said. She reached out to hold my wrist. 'Don't allow Tony Buttons to take away this moment. You understand?'

'Me understand.'

'Also,' she added, 'you must inform your teammates of your situation. You can't hide it any more.'

'Do me have to?'

'Yes, Kadeen. It's the right ting to do.'

'But . . . but me don't want to go over it again.'

I tried to block it out, but I couldn't help seeing Edson's body on the ground. A shallow pool of blood. People jostling to look. The shadow of the downtown clocktower in Old Harbour.

In the back of my mind, the prospect of identifying Tony Buttons in a Jamaican police station nagged me. It wouldn't go away.

'All right,' Aunt Mel said. 'Let me call Coach Francis. I will explain everyting.'

'You sure?'

'Yes, me sure. It's highly unlikely that anybody connected to Tony Buttons read the report, but all it takes is a Google search.'

'That's what me say to meself.'

'But me don't want this Tony Buttons dictating your life. You know, stopping you from doing the tings you enjoy. No sah!'

I tasted Aunt Mel's soup. The herbs and the spices she used filled my belly with warmness. The mutton was cooked just right. The yams and dumplings reminded me of back home.

'When you finish your dinner,' Aunt Mel said, 'go and call your father. He texted me today saying he hasn't heard from you for a liccle while.'

'That was me plan.' I nodded.

Half an hour later I called Dad. I told him about my hat-trick. 'Woi yoi!' he shouted. 'Me always thought me had a footballing superstar on our hands. Next stop is the World Cup.'

'Slow down, Dad,' I said. 'Me only playing in the South London Women's League. A mighty long way to go before me start tinking about World Cups.'

'Start believing, Kadeen!'

I also informed him how I spent my money on Louella's new boots and shin pads for me.

'You buy this Louella a pair of new boots?' He raised his voice. 'The money was for just you. That's what me working for. Couldn't this white girl afford her own boots?'

'Me don't tink so,' I replied.

'Your mother always used to complain that me never give enough for you. Now when me give you someting, you give it away!'

'Dad . . . Dad. If you did see the smile 'pon her face when she opened the box. Trust me, you woulda sing out loud.'

'White girls don't need handouts inna England.'

'Some do, Dad,' I replied. 'Around Brixton, they have

many projects and council estates where poor people live. In the news, all people talk about is the cost-of-living crisis. It takes a big bag of money just to keep your place warm. And trust me, the heat is definitely needed. England cold like penguin beak!'

Silence. *He's tinking about someting.*

'It was a godly ting to do, Kadeen,' Dad said after a short while. 'Yes, a godly ting to do. Edson will be smiling at you from heaven.'

'Me know, Dad. Me know.'

'Me was tinking,' Dad said. 'When you finally come back to Jamaica, maybe you can stay wid me for a while?'

'Jamaica? Can we talk about that another time?' I replied. 'All me can tink about is getting off that plane and going straight to the police station to identify Tony Buttons.'

'When they set the date, I'd be happy to go wid you,' offered Dad.

'Yes, me would like that. Thank you, Dad.'

I finished the call feeling a little better.

Me just wish Dad could accompany me to me next game here in South London.

26

SW2s v Croydon Tigers

The following Sunday, we made our journey south through West Norwood and South Norwood, and arrived at Croydon Stadium. One side of the ground was covered by three little stands. It wasn't Wembley, but I closed my eyes and imagined it to be. A running track ringed the pitch, which was green and level. They had marked out the centre circle and penalty areas with fresh white paint. Floodlights were in each corner of the ground.

Oh, my gosh, if me score here, it'll be mega-awesome!

'They've got proper showers and changing rooms,' said Louella. 'The water's hot! When the game is done, I'm gonna clean my boots here. I should've brought the rest of my laundry.'

'Emma!' I said. 'You can sit in the stands. Me never thought me would be saying that to you.'

'Mum just texted me,' Emma said. 'She's making fried dumplings and scrambled eggs.'

'Something to look forward to when you get home,' Coach Francis said.

'I wanted it before I stepped out. I love my fried dumplings.'

We entered the belly of the main stand and headed for the away dressing room. When we reached it, Maria was stretched out along a bench. Her eyes were closed and her arms folded. She had already changed into her kit. *Sleeping Boots*. '*Buenos días*,' she greeted.

'And good morning to you,' said Coach Francis. 'If it's all right with you, can you get up? We have quite an important game going on today.'

Maria laughed and then placed a tracksuit top over her face.

Hee Yan had also arrived early. Dressed in her kit, she performed a range of leg stretches. A green hairband tied her hair. 'Hi, Kadeen, hi, Louella. Big game today. Must win.'

'Morning, Hee Yan,' greeted Coach Francis. 'How's that engine of yours?'

'Engine is good,' Hee Yan replied. 'Revving to go.'

Blanka, Bernice and Dionne arrived next. Zoe, Neesha and Paula walked in five minutes later, followed by Yolanda and Tracey.

When everyone was ready, Coach Francis addressed the team. 'I just want to give you a heads-up about Kadeen's situation.'

The Girl With the Red Boots

She told them about what happened to Edson, why I had arrived in the UK, and to be cautious about anyone asking about me. When she had finished, everyone huddled together and raised my arm.

'If they trouble one of we,' Tracey chanted, 'then they trouble all of we!'

Everyone cheered.

'No worry,' Maria said, now fully awake. '*Te cuidaremos.*'

'What does that mean?' I asked.

'We'll look after you.'

I had to stop myself from crying.

I checked the laces on my boots before I ran out. Coach Francis walked towards me.

Oh, no, me know that sympathetic look.

'Kadeen,' she said. 'I'm still going to use you as an impact substitute.'

'Substitute!' I repeated. 'Are you serious? Me scored a hat-trick last week!'

'Yes, you've done brilliantly. I don't think any fourteen-year-old has scored a hat-trick in our league before.'

'Then why me a sub?'

'Your fitness levels,' Coach Francis replied. 'Towards the end of the game, you were blowing hard. You're not fit enough to last a whole match yet. In the summer, if you're still with us, we'll build up your stamina.'

I shook my head.

'Me can't believe this,' I whispered to myself.

'You have a future in this game,' Coach Francis added.

SW2s v Croydon Tigers

'A big future. But you must be fit to play the whole game. I haven't got the luxury of having two subs.'

Blanka led the players out. 'Let's marmalise them, mince them and dice them!'

'Let's also be composed when the chances come,' added Coach Francis.

I sulked and remained on the bench. Louella returned. 'Come on, Kadeen. Remember we're a team, and you're part of it. We're going for the league this year. Come on! I'm sure Coach Francis will put you on at half-time.'

I jogged on to the pitch with Louella. First thing I noticed was there were about eighty or ninety spectators. Maybe a hundred.

'Nuff people watching us today,' I said.

'The Kadeen effect,' grinned Louella.

I spotted Emma in the stands and waved to her as I joined the warm-up routine.

The match started. The Croydon Tigers were kitted out in orange shirts and black shorts. They weren't as ancient as the Pensioners, but they were bigger.

Lord gosh Almighty! What do they feed dem on inna England?

From the very first minute, it was clear that Croydon Tigers just wanted to defend and had no interest in attack. Coach Francis ran up and down the touchline trying to inspire our team. Midway through the first half, Dionne smacked the crossbar with a header. A few minutes later, Tracey nutmegged one of their central defenders but was denied a goal by an agile save from their goalkeeper. 'Keep it going!' yelled Coach Francis. 'Be patient, the opportunities will come.'

Just before half-time, Paula got into an argument with a spectator. She collected the ball for a throw-in and walked over to the fan. 'That's the third time you've asked,' she said. 'Mind your friggin' business!'

The man she beefed with was a black guy sitting in the front row of the main stand about thirty metres away from me. He seemed to be on his own. He wore a thick black anorak. A black scarf wrapped his neck and chin just below his mouth. His complexion was dark chocolate. He was bald. He didn't look any older than thirty. 'Me can't ask question?' he said. 'Me just asking which one of you is Kadeen. That's why me come down to watch.'

He had a Jamaican accent. Something rumbled in my belly. It wasn't the Sunday morning frost that chilled my spine. *A bredren of Tony Buttons?* I gripped the corners of my seat. I sensed my heartbeat in my throat. I turned my back on the man, willing him to go away. He didn't.

'Can't a man come and watch a game of women's football and ask a simple question?' the man added.

Paula swapped a look with Coach Francis. Blanka came rushing out of her goal to confront the spectator. *'I'm Kadeen Best,'* she shouted.

'No,' Tracey interrupted. 'I'm Kadeen Best!'

'They're all wrong,' yelled Maria, who had run over to the touchline. 'I'm Kadeen Best.'

'They're lying!' roared Yolanda. 'I'm Kadeen Best.'

SW2s v Croydon Tigers

'Don't believe them,' Zoe ranted. 'I'm Kadeen Best!'

'I'm Kadeen Best!' yelled Hee Yan in her South Korean accent.

Someone in the crowd laughed.

The man shook his head. 'Me just wanted to know who the new superstar of the South London Women's League is,' said the man. 'That's all. Play your foolish game. Me gone!'

The man stood up from his seat, cursed a few badwords and left. I breathed a little easier. My grip on my seat loosened. I stood up to stretch my legs. The referee blew her whistle. 'Play on,' she said. 'Play on!'

Coach Francis sidled up to me. 'Are you gonna be all right, Kadeen?'

I wasn't sure if I was all right.

'Me . . . me tink so.'

'Do you think you can come on for the second half?'

'Yes.' I nodded. 'Of course.'

Truth is, me would feel safer on the pitch than in the stands.

A few moments later, the referee blew the half-time whistle. I couldn't remember too much of what Coach Francis had instructed in the break. All I could think of was that this man could be connected to Tony Buttons and having to identify Tony Buttons in Jamaica.

The second half started. I spent more time checking the stands than watching the football. The man hadn't returned.

He might be waiting for me in the car park. He might be up high somewhere, aiming his gun at me.

The Girl With the Red Boots

Fifteen minutes in, Coach Francis asked me to warm up. I jogged along the touchline. There was still no sign of the guy who Paula had a row with. I should've felt more at ease, but I didn't.

Five minutes later, I replaced Yolanda. She gave me a warm hug. 'Tear them up, Kadeen,' she said. 'Score another hat-trick.'

The first time I received the ball, I had an opportunity to set Tracey free. I overhit my pass. I didn't hear it, but I knew Tracey cursed under her breath. A few minutes later, Paula found me on the wing with a good pass. I tried to go on the outside of the defender, but she stuck out a leg and won the ball.

'Head up, Kadeen,' Coach Francis yelled. 'Don't forget to chase back when you lose possession.'

Ten minutes later, we won a corner. Time was running out. Maria sprinted to take it. Bernice, Dionne, Louella and even Zoe went up for it. We desperately needed a goal. I positioned myself just outside the penalty area, in the middle of the D. Maria curled in the corner. The goalkeeper managed to get a fist to it. A defender tried to hook it further clear, but it hit the head of her own player and looped over to me. I was fifteen metres out. I had a sight of the goal.

This is the moment.

I didn't catch the ball too well. It sliced off the outside of my boot and the ball went woefully wide. It almost hit the corner flag. Goal kick. I ran back to my position on the right wing.

SW2s v Croydon Tigers

That was embarrassing.

I tried to avoid the looks from my teammates.

'Kadeen!' Coach Francis shouted. 'Keep on getting in the right positions; don't be afraid to shoot. Don't hide from the play. Head up!'

Three minutes to go.

Paula found me with another great pass. I had room to work in. This time I got the better of the left full back by cutting inside of her. I raced into the penalty area. I looked up and spotted Tracey hot-stepping towards the goal. She was unmarked. 'Kadeen!' she screamed.

The goalkeeper had come out to block a shot from me. The angle for a strike at goal wasn't good. Just as I was about to pass to Tracey, my back leg was clipped. I tumbled over. My right cheek kissed the ground.

Penalty!

The referee blew her whistle and pointed to the spot. The Croydon Tigers didn't protest. I didn't want to take this one. *No way.* Maria picked up the ball. I glanced behind me. Coach Francis had her back on the game. She couldn't watch. Emma placed her hands together as if she was in prayer. Hee Yan had turned around to face her own goal.

Carefully placing the ball on the penalty spot, Maria took a few breaths. She looked up and stared at the goalkeeper. The goalkeeper glared back. I glanced at Tracey. She stared blankly ahead at the goal, muttering something to herself. I side-eyed Paula. She gazed at the heavens.

The Girl With the Red Boots

Oh, my gosh, get this over and done wid. Me can't take the tension.

We couldn't afford to draw this game. If the Mitcham Royals won theirs, their hands would be on the title.

Maria took six paces back. Then another. The referee blew her whistle. Maria jogged up to the ball. *Is she being too casual?* It was like slow motion. She reached the ball. The strike was a solid one. *Boof!* Taking a guess, the goalkeeper dived to her right. Maria had smashed the ball into the centre of the net.

Goal!

I'm not sure how Blanka reached Maria first, but she did. She almost buried her into the pitch with her bear hug. We all dived on top. Relief flooded my veins. I heard Coach Francis in the background. 'Get back into your positions. Heads up. Concentrate!'

We jogged back into our own half. Blanka clenched a fist. 'Come on!' she roared.

A minute later, I intercepted a pass and dribbled down into the opposition's corner. Tackles came flying in, but I had used up a good thirty seconds. Coach Francis clapped. 'Well done, Kadeen. Well played.'

The Croydon Tigers had a throw-in deep inside their half, but they hardly had time to take it. The referee blew the final whistle. Strange emotions ricocheted inside me. We were one game away from winning the league. I was on the verge of claiming a liccle gold trophy. But the man in the stands could have been a bredren of Tony Buttons.

SW2s v Croydon Tigers

Why was he so eager to watch me play?

I was the first to step off the pitch. I made it inside the changing rooms and took a few deep breaths. Louella came in next. She smiled at me for a long moment before she said anything.

'I thought that one was getting away from us,' she said. 'I think our name's on that title.'

Blanka came in with the rest of my teammates. '*Our* name is on that title. Believe it!'

When we had changed, Coach Francis stood on a bench. Before she spoke, she searched our eyes and picked her moment. 'One game away,' she said. 'That's all, one game away. Whatever happens, I'm proud of you all. Proud of the way you keep going. Last year we would've got downhearted and lost a game like today's. But not today. Not this week and *not* this bloody year!'

'We're the SW2s,' Blanka chanted.

'And we haven't come this far to lose!' my teammates sang.

'And we're gonna give Mitcham Royals . . .' Blanka responded.

'The blues!'

'*Campeón de la liga!*' chanted Maria.

This time I joined in. '*Campeón de la liga!*'

'Don't celebrate until you've won the damn thing,' said Coach Francis. 'Next week will be even harder. You'll have less of the ball. You'll have to concentrate more in defence. You're gonna have to earn your doughnuts.'

The Girl With the Red Boots

Everyone prepared to leave. Coach Francis stepped towards me. She gave a half-smile.

'That guy,' I said. 'He . . . he might be a bredren of Tony Buttons.'

'And he might not,' replied Coach Francis. 'He might've been a spectator who had seen the report of last week's game and wanted to watch you play.'

'But . . . but . . .'

'Unless the police question him, we'll never know,' Coach Francis said. 'But don't you think it's highly unlikely that he'd harm you with all the other spectators watching? There must've been over a hundred in attendance. I'm sure all of them had phones to record anything if they needed to.'

I dropped my head. 'And me play so bad,' I admitted.

'You're fourteen, Kadeen,' Coach Francis said. 'You played out of your skin last week. We don't expect that every week. You're still developing. You think you played bad, but you created the penalty situation.'

'You tink so?'

'You were bright enough to think on your feet and beat the defender on her inside. Taking the ball on your left foot surprised her. She thought you were all right foot. The only way she could stop you from setting up a goal was by tripping you. Come to think of it, the ref should've sent her off. It was a clear goal-scoring opportunity.'

'That penalty was nerve-wracking,' I said.

'I couldn't watch,' Coach Francis admitted. 'I closed my eyes and waited for Blanka's roar.'

SW2s v Croydon Tigers

I laughed. 'She can roar a bit.'

'She certainly can.'

'Hee Yan does the same thing,' said Coach Francis. 'She watches for Blanka's response.'

Coach Francis put her arm around my shoulders. 'Come on, let's drive you home. Remember, you made your contribution. Sometimes it doesn't have to be hat-tricks and dribbles where you go past five players like Georgie Best.'

'Who's Georgie Best?' I wondered.

'Georgie Best?' Coach Francis repeated. 'Way before your time. He was probably the most skilful football player the UK has ever produced. And he had the same surname as you. That's gotta mean something.'

'Me will YouTube him.'

'Yes, you do that.'

We walked out of the ground. I looked here and there. There was no sign of the man who wanted to watch me play. I felt safer as I climbed into the back seat of Coach Francis' car next to Emma. Louella was already in the front passenger seat. 'One game away from glory,' she said. 'I hope they buff up the little gold cups proper before they give them to us. It's gonna look sweet on my dressing table.'

'*Don't* tempt fate,' warned Coach Francis. 'We're going to have to play our best game of the season to beat the Royals.'

'Are they really that good?' I asked.

Coach Francis didn't answer. Instead, she swapped a look with Louella.

'And if that same guy who was asking about you turns up and starts harassing you, we'll chase him out of South London,' Louella promised.

I smiled. It was nice I had the back-up of my teammates.

27

The Chess Strategy

Emma and I had just finished school chess club. I played my very first match against Nuno Figo. He didn't say much. He just had this intense stare on the board when he was deciding to make a move. He beat me in fifteen minutes.

'You must support your pawns,' he advised after the game. 'They're just as important as any other piece.'

'OK.' I nodded.

'Better luck next time.'

'Luck?' Miss Jackson repeated. She had been walking around the classroom, checking on games. She watched the conclusion of my match. 'There is no such thing as luck. Just the application of hard work and concentration.'

As it was a sunny, crisp day, Emma and I decided to take the long walk home. We turned left into Railton Road, stepped to the end of the street and made our way into

The Girl With the Red Boots

Brockwell Park. People walked their dogs. Parents pushed their buggies. A few runners and cyclists went by. Some kid was trying to fly a dragon kite. I felt a calmness here out of the hustle and bustle of downtown Brixton. I imagined I was making my way barefoot along Old Harbour Bay, the warm, gentle waves soothing my toes.

'Nuno said to me, me must support my pawns,' I said. 'But a pawn is not as powerful as a queen or even a knight.'

'They're still important,' said Emma. 'If you didn't have any pawns to start a game, you'd never win a match.'

'OK. That makes sense.'

'Your opponent is always looking for a weakness,' Emma continued. 'Even if it's a pawn without any back-up. You can't send your pawn into battle without back-up.'

'Me tink me beginning to understand.'

'Just don't leave any of your pawns on their lonesome,' Emma added. 'Treat them like they're as important as any other piece. It's like in football. If you have a slow defender, then a midfield player will come and help that defender when they're under attack, right?'

'Right,' I agreed.

'Remember that for your next game,' Emma said. 'You're getting better.'

'Nuno still beat me in fifteen minutes,' I laughed.

'When I first joined, everyone was beating me in ten minutes,' Emma admitted. 'Sometimes even less. Miss Jackson used to ask if I was all right after every game.'

We walked uphill along a path that led to the Tulse Hill

exit of the park. We could just about see the skyscrapers of Central London. I sniffed something foul from the nearby pond.

'Got some good news,' Emma said.

'What's that?'

'I'll be going to see my dad in the summer holidays.'

'That's . . . that's mega-epic,' I said.

'But Mum won't be coming with me. I'll be going on my lonesome. Dad's gonna link me at the airport. I'm gonna stay with his family near Saint Ann's Bay.'

'Why can't your mum go?'

'Can't afford to at the moment,' Emma said. 'Flights to Jamaica in the summer are proper expensive.'

'Can't you go any other time?'

'Nope,' Emma replied. 'Mum might get slapped with a fine if she takes me out of school.'

'Is the fine bigger than the cost of a summertime flight?' I asked.

Emma thought about it. 'That's a good question. Mum and I will do the maths.'

'When me get back to Jamaica, me might be staying wid me dad in Montego Bay,' I said. 'So if you're in Saint Ann's Bay, we could link up. Both places are on the north coast.'

'Definitely!' Emma nodded. Her face lit up.

'Maybe me will get me dad to pick you up and bring you back to Montego Bay. We'll show you around and then have a dip in the sea.'

'We'll be like holiday sisters,' Emma said.

'Yes, me always wanted a sister,' I agreed. 'And me must introduce you to me good friends Sienna and Melody. Trust me, they will make you laugh.'

'That's a deal,' said Emma. 'I can't wait.'

28

A View to Thrill

On Thursday, just after 4 p.m., I had arrived home and settled down in my room to catch up on some history homework. I had let my schoolwork drift a bit. In my last phone call with Mum, she had gone on forever about how I must be ready and prepped to sit for the Caribbean Secondary Education Certificate. She reminded me that many children of my age in Jamaica do not get the opportunity for further education because their parents cannot afford the textbooks.

Gosh! So many young lives lost in the Second World War. Me granny tell me that Jamaican airmen fought in that conflict, but there is nothing in me textbook about dem.

The doorbell rang.

Who could that be? Aunt Mel didn't tell me she was expecting any delivery. Surely it could not be the man who was looking for me at the football? Me good heart banged a liccle quicker. Should me answer it?

Before I opened the front door, I pulled back a net curtain to spy out a front window. It was Louella. *Relief.* She was still in her school uniform.

What's she doing here?

I opened the door.

'Kadeen! I'm glad you're in.'

'Louella. Good to see you. What brings you to me door?'

'Didn't I say I was gonna treat you?'

'Er . . . yes, you did say that.'

'Today's the day. Come, put your shoes on. I'm taking you somewhere.'

'Where?'

'You'll see.'

I pulled on my red Puma trainers and my jacket. Louella led me to Brixton Tube station. She had a bounce in her stride, and I had to skip to keep up.

'You're taking me uptown?' I asked.

Louella grinned. She gave me an Oyster card to get through the ticket barrier.

We changed at Stockwell to get on the Northern line. We finally got off at Battersea Power Station.

'Shopping?' I asked. 'Aunt Mel told me she'd been shopping here once but they have plenty expensive name-brand stores. "They're not getting me good money," she's always saying.'

'No shopping,' Louella replied.

A View to Thrill

We entered the Battersea Power Station complex; the four chimneys almost kissed the clouds. I couldn't work it out. *If we're not shopping, then what?*

Maybe she's taking me for someting to eat? Yes, that must be it. Me never sampled an Indian meal before. It could be that. Or an Italian! Me would love to try a pasta dish one day wid spicy meatballs. You can't get that in Old Harbour.

We took the escalator to the first floor. I was still baffled.

There was a queue of people waiting to go through a ticket barrier. Behind it, in white lights fixed against a wall, was *Lift 109*.

'What's Lift 109?'

'It's a lift that goes straight up through a chimney,' replied Louella.

'One of dem chimney?' I repeated. 'They built a lift in there?'

'Yep,' said Louella. 'They sure did. When you get to the top, it shows you an epic view of all over London.'

'You serious? Is it safe? Me don't want to end me life dropping down a long chimney. It's going to be a big mess at the bottom.'

'Of course it's safe. It's a new tourist attraction. Before we arrived at training yesterday, the girls got together. Everyone contributed. We thought that you hadn't seen everything in London yet, so we come up with this idea.'

'Thanks,' I said.

'The other idea was a visit to London Zoo,' said Louella. 'But I hate to see animals behind bars. Mum's always saying that zoos would become more popular if it was politicians who were forced to live there.'

Ten minutes later we went through the security gates. *Could they really build a lift in an ancient chimney?*

In the waiting area, there were old black-and-white photographs and text displays of how the now-closed Battersea Power Station was built and how much of London it provided electricity for. They used untold coal. Didn't see too many black people in those pics. It must've been before the *Empire Windrush* and all that.

A guide led us into the lift. Twenty or so people stepped in with us. I held on to a bar, but it was a smooth ride. We arrived at the top. Suddenly natural light hit our faces. *Oh, my gosh! A mega-awesome view.* I could see the Wembley Arch right down to the Crystal Palace towers and everything in between. I could make out Buckingham Palace, the London Eye and the Tower of London. The bends and curves in the River Thames were more obvious up here than on ground level. It was like I was in a plane, but the pilot had put it on pause. I gazed towards Brixton and wondered if Aunt Mel had finished work for the day. *Has she seen this view yet?* I took untold pics and selfies. *Me can't wait to send dem to Sienna and Melody.*

Louella must've seen my joy. 'The girls and I thought that you could do with a treat after the scare you had last Sunday, you know, with that mouthy guy.'

'Thanks so much,' I said. 'This is seriously impressive. Me never been up so high inna building in all me days.'

For five minutes or so, I watched London. Then I closed my eyes and dreamed a little.

Could me live here sometime in the future? Could me be a professional footballer one day? Me at the top. Playing at Wembley Stadium. Scoring a hat-trick there. Why not? No Tony Buttons or any of him bredren are going to put me off. Yes, sah! Me can't lie. Me did like the feeling reading me very name in the newspaper did give me. Maybe me can be famous one day wearing me red boots.

'Louella,' I said. 'Me ready for Sunday.'

'I'm ready too,' she said. 'I played well in my new boots.'

'And me not going to change me red ones,' I said. 'They bring me luck.'

'Glad you liked the treat,' Louella said.

I looked out over South London once again. 'Me love it.' I nodded. 'Love it to the bone.'

29

SW2s v Mitcham Royals

The following Saturday evening, Aunt Mel had cooked a delishi-ocious chicken stir-fry meal mixing peppers, spring onions, sweetcorn, mushrooms and noodles. I had nearly finished my plate when I thought of something.

'Why don't you come and watch me play tomorrow?' I asked. 'We're in April now. Icicles are no longer hanging off me nose-bridge. It's the last game of the season and we have a chance of winning the league.'

Aunt Mel sipped her glass of water. In the last couple of weeks or so, I had noticed she drank more water than sparkling wine.

'Me don't tink so,' Aunt Mel replied. 'Me don't understand football. Sometimes the referee blow their whistle and me don't know why dem blowing it for. Take, for instance, the offside rule. Me had an ex-boyfriend trying to explain it to me. He might as well have been trying to teach me nuclear physics.'

'Can't you come, Aunt Mel? Just this once. It's me last game.'

Aunt Mel twirled noodles around her fork and half smiled. She nibbled a piece of chicken and swallowed it. 'OK, but please don't expect me to talk football tactics wid anyone. Me just coming to support you . . . if it don't rain.'

'That's all me want,' I said. 'That's enough. You have been great wid me since me come here.'

'And you have been great company,' Aunt Mel said. 'Me can't lie. It does get lonely for me sometime.'

'You'll find someone soon,' I said.

'It's not a man I crave for,' Aunt Mel explained. 'Me miss family and friends, you know. In the winter here, people don't go out too much. They go to work, go home and find someting to watch on the TV. That's it. In Jamaica, you can socialise when you want to at any time of the year. I miss that kinda lifestyle.'

'So you're going home?'

'At first, me will take a six-week break just to see how me feel in Jamaica. Me will check the job situation.'

'Where will you stay?'

'Me did talk about this wid your mother last night.'

'What did she say?'

Aunt Mel sucked in a breath.

'If it's all right, me would like to stay wid you and your

mother,' she said. 'Just until me find me feet, you know, get a job and can find a place for myself.'

'That's good wid me.' I nodded. 'No problem. Me do have one condition though.'

'Oh, what's that?' Aunt Mel asked. She angled her eyebrows and scratched her nose.

'That you will make this chicken stir-fry when you decide to cook.'

Aunt Mel rocked back in her seat and laughed hard. Her cheeks burst into life. 'Oh, Kadeen! You make me fret for a second. Bless you. Of course! Chicken stir-fry it is.'

'What's the name of the sauce?'

'Oh, that's my secret recipe!'

The next day. Sunday.

England is very strange. Just two weeks ago, me shiver when me coming outta me front door. Now there is not a cloud in the sky, birds are singing, and me didn't need me thick anorak to step outside. Just me tracksuit top.

Despite the warmer weather, Aunt Mel had made herself a flask of coffee. She had checked the weather forecast for rain. Emma and Aunt Mel were chatting in the kitchen as I rubbed Vaseline over my red boots. 'Don't let me down today,' I said to them. 'You see how me keep you clean and well greased? Make me score another hat-trick today. Mitcham Royals, here me come.'

Five minutes later, we heard Coach Francis' car horn.

Aunt Mel and I squeezed into the back seats with Emma.

SW2s v Mitcham Royals

Almost immediately, Aunt Mel sneezed. She gave me a look. 'Cats?' she whispered.

I nodded.

'Great that you're coming to support, Mel,' Coach Francis greeted. 'We're gonna need it. We're playing at the Royals' home ground on Wimbledon Common.'

'Is that near where they play tennis?' I asked.

'Not too far away,' Louella replied. 'Asked to join a tennis club near there once. But it's just too damn expensive.'

As we neared Wimbledon Common, my nerves took a lift to the ninth floor. The car park, close to the changing rooms, was ram-jammed. I helped Coach Francis take out the balls from the boot of her car. Emma collected the first-aid kit and the half-time oranges. 'I'm going to use you again as an impact substitute, Kadeen,' Coach Francis said. 'Be on your toes, as I might put you on early today.'

'Me will be ready.'

Coach Francis turned to Aunt Mel. 'We're playing on pitch number three.'

'OK. Good luck, Kadeen, Louella. Score a whole heap of goals if you can.'

Aunt Mel made her way to pitch number three and the rest of us headed to the changing rooms.

Maria had already changed into her kit. She wasn't sleeping. This time she sat on a bench, nervously tapping her feet. I thought she might wear out her studs. Bernice and Dionne had arrived early too. They tied and checked

The Girl With the Red Boots

their bootlaces. Hee Yan, dressed in our colours, read some thick book about criminal law.

Me guess everyone prepares for big games in their own way.

Ten minutes later, the team were kitted and booted. Coach Francis stood on a wooden chair to deliver her team talk.

'You have done so well to keep up with the Royals this season,' she said. 'They haven't been beaten on these grounds for nearly two years, but all unbeaten runs come to an end. Let us be the ones to inflict that pain on them.'

'Great pain on them!' blurted out Blanka.

'Don't let fear of losing affect your performance,' resumed Coach Francis. 'Express yourselves the way you want to. Defend and attack as a unit. Play for each other. Play for your girlfriends, boyfriends, mums and dads and anyone else who supported you in your football career. I'm convinced you can beat them. Go out there and do it!'

'Who are we?' Blanka roared.

'The SW2s!'

'And we never . . .'

'Lose!'

Before we trotted out, I stood on a bench. 'Just want to say thanks for the treat of Lift 109,' I said. 'Me had a great time wid Louella, and the view was incredible.'

'We were thinking of sending you to the Tower of London's dungeon after you missed that chance last week,' Tracey joked. 'I've been up Lift 109 myself. It's a wicked view.'

'When you return to Jamaica,' Paula said, 'we're expecting an invitation to all the top reggae beach parties and dances, and backstage passes to reggae concerts.'

'But . . . but . . . me don't know any famous singer,' I said. 'Me can show you where Beenie Man live.'

Everyone laughed.

'She's joking with you,' said Neesha. 'Pay us back by banging in six goals when you come on today.'

Pitch number three was about five hundred metres away from the changing rooms. There must have been around one hundred and fifty people already waiting on the sidelines.

The title decider. This game is massive.

Neatly cut grass pretty much covered the whole pitch except the areas around the six-yard box at both ends. Purple-coloured nets hung behind the goalposts. Purple and white flags fluttered atop the corner poles.

Something else caught my eye. Close to the halfway line was a long table with a red tablecloth. Resting on one end of it was a gold cup about fifty centimetres high, sitting on what looked like a black onyx base. The sun reflected off its curve. Fourteen replica gold cups, the size of wine glasses, surrounded it. At the other end of the table stood a wooden shield with a silver plaque fixed on to it. Fourteen smaller versions of this trophy kept the bigger one company. There was a woman in a long furry coat and a pair of expensive-looking Uggs standing behind the table. She was chatting to a man wearing a blue suit and holding a clipboard.

I wasn't starting the game, but my nerves had reached as high as Lift 109.

Me want to take one of dem gold liccle cups home to Jamaica.

I joined the warm-up routine.

On the other side of the pitch, the Mitcham Royals did their stretches with their purple tracksuit tops on. A three-pointed gold crown was emblazoned on to their backs. They wore white shorts, and purple-coloured socks and hairbands. They then did a quick passing routine. I can't lie. They looked very impressive to the max. *Can we really beat them?*

The referee blew her whistle. The captains came together in the centre circle and shook hands. A coin was tossed. I joined Coach Francis, Emma and Aunt Mel on the sideline.

'You're not starting?' Aunt Mel asked.

'No, that's up to the coach,' I replied.

Aunt Mel half smiled and then side-eyed Coach Francis. The match began.

The Mitcham Royals kept the ball well. All their defenders could pick a pass. We struggled to get possession in the first ten minutes, but we had the first opportunity. Bernice won a tough tackle in midfield. She fed the ball to Neesha. Neesha got the better of her marker and made her way into the Mitcham Royals' half. Yolanda called for the ball on the left wing. She received it and looked up. Tracey hotfooted into the penalty area. Yolanda delivered the ball close to the near post. Tracey beat a defender to it, but her flick grazed the outside of the post. Goal kick.

SW2s v Mitcham Royals

'That's more like it!' shouted Coach Francis. 'Great move!'

Five minutes later, the Mitcham Royals had their first chance. They played the ball through our midfield. It ended up at the feet of their striker. She hit the ball well, but it was straight at Blanka. She palmed it over the bar. Corner.

I felt the tension in my chest and decided to jog along the touchline. There was no sign of the man who had asked questions about me the previous week. *Relief.*

Back on the pitch, the Mitcham Royals were putting us under serious pressure. They had a series of corners and got four shots on goal. We couldn't get out of our own half.

'You're defending too deep!' hollered Coach Francis. 'Move up! Move up!'

A few moments later, they scored. I can't lie. It was a pretty goal. Their number ten tricked her way past Hee Yan and Paula, then made a short pass to their number nine. Their number ten received the ball again near the penalty spot and chipped it over the advancing Blanka. *Goal.* Mitcham Royals supporters on the sidelines jumped up and down, hugged each other and clapped. Blanka, shaking her head, took her own sweet time in retrieving the ball out of the net. My heart sank to between my kneecap and ankle. I stared at Coach Francis.

Put me on now! Please put me on now!

Coach Francis only had eyes for the game. She ignored me and watched the restart.

The Girl With the Red Boots

I glanced across to the man standing beside the trophy table. He wrote something down on his clipboard.

Maybe me will have to satisfy meself wid the small silver shield.

Their goal seemed to slap the confidence out of us. They had three more opportunities to strike again. We managed to keep the score down to a single goal as the referee blew for half-time. Coach Francis turned to me. 'Kadeen, warm up. I'm putting you on.'

I did my stretches and jogged along the touchline as Coach Francis turned up her vocals on my teammates. I had never seen her so vex.

'You're treating the ball like a hot potato,' she said. 'You can't wait to get rid of it. The ball's your friend, not your enemy. Composure! And you're treating them with too much respect. They're not Real Madrid! You must show more composure on the ball. And *don't* dive in on their number ten. Watch the ball when you tackle her. Don't give her so much room.'

I replaced Yolanda. She gave me a hug and a high-five. 'Kill them with your speed, Kadeen.'

'Me will try.'

For the first ten minutes of the second half, we had to defend. I spent more time in my own penalty area than theirs. I had hardly touched the ball. Suddenly they misplaced a pass and I intercepted it in midfield. I surged past one of their midfielders and raced into the space on the left wing. Tracey tried to keep up. Their right back was out of position. A central defender moved out to confront me but I easily passed her on my outside. I approached the goal-line. Tracey screamed for the ball.

Can me trust me left foot? Me don't want to mess this up. Edson had always drilled into me to practise with my weaker side.

I crossed the ball with my left. It wasn't perfect. The ball went over at waist height. Tracey's diving header was brave and incredible. She just launched herself at the ball. The goalkeeper didn't even move.

Goal!

Tracey got up to her feet, clenched her fists and punched the air. 'Yessssss!'

Without hesitation, I jumped on to her back. I don't know how she didn't topple over. Blanka arrived to celebrate next. They did this chest-bump thing that would've caused injury to me if I tried it. 'What a super-doolooping-frigging-header!'

I hoped someone caught that on their mobile phone.

Coach Francis pointed to her temples. 'Concentrate!' she yelled. 'Composure! Be confident on the ball. Don't give it away.'

It was tiring trying to get the ball off the Royals. They pinned us back into our own half and we had rare opportunities to attack. They played pretty football, but they couldn't turn their possession of the ball into goals. Louella, Bernice, Dionne, Zoe and Hee Yan were always there with a tackle or a last-ditch block to keep the score one-one.

The Girl With the Red Boots

Five minutes to go. We had to score another.

They had a corner. Coach Francis had told me to stay up the pitch on the halfway line. 'Stay on the shoulder of the last defender,' she instructed. 'But don't get caught offside.'

Dionne managed to get her head to the corner. Louella booted the ball upfield. It looked like the ball was bouncing out for a throw-in, but I switched on my zoomers and managed to keep the ball in play. The centre back had followed me. She was exposed and had no one to support her. I remembered what Nuno and Emma taught me about supporting all your pieces in chess. I approached the defender with the ball, performing three step overs before I passed her on her inside. I raced towards the goal. I looked up, but this time Tracey hadn't kept up with my pace. One defender stood between me and the goal. I cut back on to my right foot, and then on to my left. The centre back kept her eyes on the ball. I slowed down just a touch then quick-toed past her. I glanced up again. The goalkeeper stood on the six-yard line. She readied herself for the shot, spreading her arms. I decided to blast the ball as hard as I could.

Get your knee over the ball, I remember Edson repeating to me as he taught me how to shoot. *You don't want the ball to fly high over the bar.*

Boof! I struck the ball sweeter than any shot I've hit in my life. It smashed against the crossbar and looped back into play. Once again, the goalkeeper didn't even move.

Tracey had finally caught up with the attack. She reached the dropping ball first and nodded it into the net before the goalkeeper could fist it clear.

Goallllllll!

The celebrations went on for a long minute. I thought Blanka might have injured Tracey, but she didn't care. Instead of telling us to get back into our positions, Coach Francis did a liccle dance on the touchline and pumped her fists. Emma and Aunt Mel jumped, cheered and clapped.

The game finally restarted. I defended like never before. I slid in here and there and blocked three shots. Mud covered my shorts and half of my shirt.

One minute to go. I was exhausted. The Royals launched yet another attack on our right side. Their left winger nutmegged me and zoomed towards our goal. I chased after her in one last weary sprint. I mistimed the tackle.

Oh, no! What have me done?

The Royals screamed for a penalty, but the referee said the foul was committed just outside the penalty area.

That was too damn close.

We lined up a wall. I stood in the middle of it. I puffed hard. Their number ten stood behind the ball. She eyed up the top left-hand corner. If this went in, there'd be no time to respond. *The title will be lost. There'll be no liccle gold cup nicing up our house in Jamaica.* The referee blew her whistle. Their number ten took a measured run-up to the ball. *Boof.* The ball went over my head. I spun around. It arrowed towards the top-left corner of our goal. *Oh, no.* I glanced at Louella, who stood with me in the wall. I could see the dread in her face.

Suddenly, flying through the air, was Blanka. She managed to get a left palm to the ball to deflect it over the bar. 'Yessssss!' she roared. 'You're not passing me today, this week or this year!'

The Royals hurried to take a corner, but it was too late. The referee blew the full-time whistle. We all rushed towards Blanka and leapt on top of her. I think I received more bruises from that celebration than from any bad tackle.

'*Campeón de la Liga*,' Maria chanted.

'*CAMPEÓN de la LIGA!*'

It was an incredible feeling. Our supporters ran on to the pitch. Some laughed. Some cried. Others didn't know what to do with themselves. Maria, Hee Yan and Neesha dropped to their knees, hugging each other. Coach Francis remained still on the touchline. She looked up to the heavens and said a few silent words. To whom she spoke, I didn't know.

Ten minutes later, I learned that the lady who stood by the trophy table was a Ms Rachel George MBE. I had never heard of her, but apparently she once played for Arsenal and won five FA Cups and three league titles. The man with her was the President of the South London Women's League, a Mr Kenny Wright. They shook the hands of our opponents and presented them with their runners-up trophy. Every single Royals player looked like they were about to cry puddles. Their manager, his arms pointing this way and that, complained to the referee about something.

Then it was our turn. Blanka already had a bottle of Prosecco in her hands. *Where did that come from?* The crowd converged. There must have been about two hundred people watching.

'And now if I can ask the SW2s to step up and collect the South London Women's Championship cup and their individual trophies,' Rachel George said.

Led by Blanka and Maria, we received the gold and our individual bling to roars of acclaim.

'*CAMPEÓN de la LIGA! CAMPEÓN de la LIGA!*'

We jumped up and down as friends, relatives and spectators took their pics. For a short moment, I studied my cup. On its base it had a little black plaque with the words *Champions of the South London Women's League* engraved on to it. It was heavier than I had expected. The surge of pride I felt was overwhelming. I couldn't stop the tears rolling down my cheeks.

Yes, he'd be proud. So proud. Edson, this is for you!

Before I knew it, Aunt Mel stood in front of me with a tissue. She gently wiped my face. 'Me don't know too much about football,' she said. 'But my goodness, the Royals' defence could never catch you! They might as well have had a sack of rice tied to dem boots.'

She gazed at me for a long second before pulling me in for a hug. 'Congratulations, Kadeen. You deserve everyting you get.'

The Girl With the Red Boots

Emma was next to applaud me. 'I hope if we ever win the chess league, the cups are as nice as the one you got,' she said. 'Seriously, massive congrats. You're so quick and skilful with the ball. They couldn't lay a toe on you. You exposed their weakness on the right side of their defence.'

'Don't stop there,' I said. 'Tell me more!'

Before Emma added another word, someone else said something. I recognised *him* instantly. Everything in my body went cold. I backed away two paces and held on to my gold cup a little tighter. It was the man who came to watch me play last week. He wore the same black anorak and a sly grin. No scarf this time. He owned a square jaw. His lips were red, and his wonky teeth were stained brown.

'Me sure you will make it as a professional footballer,' he said. 'Me sure of that. But don't talk to the *wrong* people. Do you understand me? You don't want to spoil someting that's so good.'

He then turned and walked away.

My heartbeat accelerated like a plane on the runway. I stood perfectly still. It killed my moment of joy.

'Don't worry about him,' said Emma. 'He's just trying to intimidate you.'

For a long minute, I closed my eyes and tried to wish him away.

When Emma embraced me, I heard shouting and yelling. I took a step back from Emma. I spotted Coach Francis and Aunt Mel cussing the man in the black anorak in the far corner of the pitch. I couldn't hear what was being said, but the man didn't want to face up to them. His bustling stride turned into a jog. *Wow!*

Ten minutes later, Aunt Mel waited for me with Emma outside the entrance to the changing rooms. Inside, the celebrations continued. Coach Francis got christened with another bottle of bubbling Prosecco, I learned some new English, Polish, Korean and Spanish dance moves, and Tracey told me she loved me. 'You set up both of my goals,' she said. 'You're gonna make it big! You know why? Cos me say so! I can spot a real talent when I see one. Now, come and drink a cup of championship juice.'

She poured the drink into a paper cup and offered it to me. I accepted. 'You don't win a gold cup every day,' I said.

Then I sank the drink in two gulps. I felt a bit dizzy.

Oh, Lord! Better not tell Aunt Mel.

'Not so fast,' Tracey giggled. 'Not so fast! Sip it! And let me tell you something. If that pond-troll ever appears again, I'll chase him outta South London and into the river with the rest of the team.'

'Thanks,' I managed.

'Put your gold cup on display in a nice place where everyone can see it,' she said. 'You and your family deserve it.'

Suddenly I burst into tears. We shared a hug.

Me must stop crying in front of people!

Half an hour later, laden with our gold cups, Coach Francis drove us home. She, Emma and Louella stepped out of the car to walk Aunt Mel and me to our front door.

The Girl With the Red Boots

'You have a real, special talent,' Coach Francis said to me. 'You remind me of John Barnes and Laurie Cunningham.'

'I've heard of John Barnes,' I said. 'But Laurie Cunningham? Who's he?'

'Don't worry,' Coach Francis said. 'Just me showing my age again. We don't know when you'll be returning to Jamaica, but pre-season training starts in July. I'll get to work on that stamina of yours.'

'Like you said,' I replied, 'me don't know when me will return home. It could be any day now. Me just want to thank you for the opportunity to play.'

'It was my pleasure,' said Coach Francis. 'You certainly made a difference. You've earned your doughnuts. With your trickery and pace, no one can touch you.'

'Until you leave, we can still play in Brocky Park,' said Louella. 'Not in my new boots though. I'll save those for the important matches.'

'Of course,' I said. 'Just don't break me toe wid your crunchy tackling before me leave.'

Everyone hugged each other before Coach Francis, Emma and Louella returned to the car.

'*Campeón de la Liga!*' I yelled.

'*CAMPEÓN de la LIGA!*'

30

Return Flight

Over the next two weeks, I enjoyed the school Easter holidays with Louella and Emma. We stepped to the movies together, visited each other's houses, played chess and went shopping. One afternoon, I even babysat for Louella's liccle twin brothers as Louella accompanied her mum to a social security appointment. They forever begged me to give them the chocolate finger biscuits, but Louella told me they only had that treat on a weekend.

I tried my best to rid the threat of Tony Buttons and his bredren from my mind, but he was always there. His thick silver chain shining brightly from his dark neck. His bald head. His hard eyes. His goatee beard. I took that image to bed with me and it invaded my mental space when I woke up.

*

The Girl With the Red Boots

It was the first Sunday in May and I was playing another chess match with Emma at her home when Aunt Mel called me. 'Your mother and Officer Crystal Myers want to talk to you today if that's OK?'

'Yes . . . yes,' I replied. 'Me will be home in the next half an hour.'

'OK,' Aunt Mel said. 'Don't be late.'

It had taken Emma twenty-four minutes to beat me. I had even taken her queen, the first time I had done so.

'You're getting better all the time,' she said. 'Giving support to all your pieces. I've got to think hard to beat you now.'

'And me going to tink hard to beat you too,' I replied.

We both laughed.

'Once you return to Jamaica,' Emma said, 'maybe we can play matches online? There's an app we can get.'

'Yes, me good for that,' I said. 'Make sure you put in plenty practice. Me coming for you!'

I arrived home twenty minutes later. Aunt Mel sat at the kitchen table watching the news on a low volume. I parked myself opposite her and she gave me a comforting look. 'Are you ready to call your mother? The police officer is wid her. They're waiting.'

I closed my eyes for a short second and sucked in a long breath. Aunt Mel switched off the TV.

'Me ready,' I said.

Aunt Mel punched my mum's number into her phone. As it rang, I poured myself a glass of cold water.

'Hello,' Mum said. 'Is Kadeen there?'

'Yes, she is,' replied Aunt Mel. 'Hold on a sec. I'll put it on speaker.'

'Hi, Mum.'

'Kadeen. So good to hear your voice. Everyting OK wid you?'

'Not too bad,' I said. 'Sometimes it get boring now the football season done. But Louella and Emma keep me company. We went to the movies the other day at the Battersea Power Station complex.'

'Nice to hear you made some good friends,' Mum said. 'Officer Crystal Myers is wid me.'

'Hello, Kadeen,' Crystal greeted. 'Congratulations on winning the South London Women's League. Fantastic news.'

'Hi, Crystal,' I replied. 'Thank you.'

'Playing football must have been a good distraction for you,' Crystal said.

'Oh, yes,' I agreed. 'It take me mind off tings. Playing chess too.'

'Kadeen,' Crystal said. I noticed a change of tone in her voice. 'We'd like you to return to Jamaica in two weeks' time . . . if you're ready?'

'Two weeks,' I repeated. 'Me not going to finish the school year here so in London?'

'I'm afraid not,' said Mum. 'They want you to identify Tony Buttons at a Kingston police station.'

'There'll be a line-up of about six or seven men,' revealed

Crystal. 'You will be asked to identify Tony Buttons through a mirror. You can see dem but they won't be able to see you. You understand?'

'Yes . . . yes me understand.'

'It's up to you, Kadeen,' Mum said. 'If you're not ready then they can postpone it for another time.'

'We just want to gather as much evidence as we can before we charge him for your brother's murder,' added Crystal.

'Will . . . will me be alone?'

'No,' replied Mum. 'Your father and meself will be wid you.'

'And me too,' said Crystal.

'What police station do we have to go to?'

'Keep this to yourself,' warned Crystal. 'Tell nobody outside your immediate family, not even anyone in England or a long-time school friend.'

'Don't worry,' I said. 'Me want me brother's murderer to receive full justice. Make him rot inna dirty prison cell until me eye-corner turn wrinkly and crinkly.'

Aunt Mel nodded and held on to my wrist.

'The plan is to take you straight from Kingston Airport to the Pegasus Hotel on Knutsford Boulevard,' Crystal said. 'You can relax there for two days. They have a pool, a gym and tings to do to keep you occupied. I will be staying in a room next door. Then we will drive you to the new police station in Olympic Gardens. They have maximum security there. Me can assure you of that.'

Return Flight

'After the identification,' Mum said, 'your father will drive you to Montego Bay to stay wid him. Is that what you wanted?'

'Yes, Mum. It'll be good to stay wid Dad for a liccle while.'

'Is there anyting else you want to ask me while me here?' Crystal asked.

I thought about it. 'Who's going to pick me up at the airport?'

'That will be me in an unmarked police car,' Crystal replied. 'Try not to worry. Everyting will be fine.'

'It's a brave ting you're doing, Kadeen,' said Mum. 'Me will be wid Crystal to pick you up from the airport. Your father too.'

'Brave?' I repeated. 'Me just don't want any other family to suffer from bad breed people like Tony Buttons. Dem have to be taken off the streets.'

'That's why we need as much strong evidence as possible,' said Crystal. 'It will give the prosecution power to do just what you and so many ask. In the past, so many get away. *Not* this time.'

'Don't worry,' I said. 'Me still remember everyting from that day like it was yesterday.'

I paused for a moment as my mind brought up the scene of Edson lying still on the ground in the clocktower's shadow. A shudder went through me.

When will this ever stop?

'Me can't forget him,' I said. 'Make him pay for what he has done to all of we.'

'Thank you, Kadeen,' Crystal said. 'You're one courageous girl. Me can't tell you how much we appreciate this.'

A minute later, I finished the call.

Aunt Mel looked at me for a while before she said something. 'Me never been there, but me hear the Pegasus Hotel is one of Kingston's finest.'

'Why don't you come wid me?' I asked. 'Me could do wid some company on the plane.'

'It's too soon,' Aunt Mel replied. 'Me already tell your mother me will be coming in July. Hopefully tings will settle down by then.'

'Yes.' I nodded. 'Me don't need any more drama.'

'Me going to miss you, Kadeen,' Aunt Mel said. 'It was nice to come home to someone, you know, to cook for someone, share your day wid someone.'

'Me going to miss you too, Aunt Mel. Big time.'

'As you know, me don't yet understand football,' Aunt Mel said. 'But me learned someting from watching your team play.'

'Oh? What was that, Aunt Mel?'

'The teamwork,' she replied. 'The way you defended attack after attack from that team . . . what was their name?'

'Mitcham Royals.'

'Yes.' Aunt Mel nodded. 'Mitcham Royals. They put you under some heavy pressure. Everybody had to help out. Living over here so in the UK, me feel that me under serious pressure too. Me need more teamwork in me life. Someone to protect me and lift me up when me down. You understand?'

'Yes, me tink so.'

Aunt Mel squeezed my wrist again. 'Enjoy the rest of your time here, Kadeen. Maybe we can catch a play or a movie or someting before you go.'

'Me would love that,' I said. 'And me can't wait until you come back to Jamaica.'

I couldn't lie. I would not only miss Aunt Mel but Emma, Louella and my new teammates – the SW2s.

The SW2s don't come to lose!
Will I ever play with dem again?

31

Homeland

I couldn't sleep on the flight.

I had a window seat. I positioned my head this way and that, but I just couldn't get comfortable.

Aunt Mel had given me a great send-off. On my last day in Brixton she had invited Coach Francis and my teammates down for a surprise going-home party. Maria had brought her home-cooked paella and Blanka had fried these fat dumplings that she called pierogi. They were stuffed with vegetables, cheese, fruit and chocolate. I hesitated to taste, but it worked. Delishi-ocious.

'It's a traditional Polish dish,' she said. '*Piekny!* Eat some more.'

I was pretty much full before I tried Hee Yan's kimchi. She told me it was fermented vegetables with a dose of sour and spice. 'It's very good for you,' she said. 'Lots of fibre. Good for footballers.'

We took pics with the championship trophy and selfies galore. Everyone promised to visit me in Jamaica when they had the chance. Drinks flowed and jokes were laughed at. I stayed away from the Prosecco and beers.

I said a final goodbye to Louella. She was in tears before me. She held me tight for a minute or so. 'I'm going to do everything I can to visit you in Jamaica,' she said. 'I'll get a part-time job somewhere and save my money. When you get to Jamaica, spell out my name on your fave beach.'

'Will do.' I nodded.

Saying farewell to Emma was just as difficult. Few words were said. 'Me wish me could take you inna me suitcase,' I said.

'You crunch yourself in the suitcase,' she laughed. 'I'll pretend I'm you.'

We hugged and cried.

The next morning, I didn't want to leave.

Now me flying to Kingston, where me must identify Tony Buttons.

I landed at Norman Manley International Airport just outside Kingston. It was late afternoon. As others collected their cabin luggage, I remained in my seat for a few minutes. My heart punched against my ribcage. I so wanted to see my parents but I would have happily sat in my seat and waited for the plane to return to the UK.

The Girl With the Red Boots

Maybe Mum and Dad could fly to the UK. Maybe me could identify Tony Buttons via Zoom or someting?

I was one of the last to leave the plane. 'Have a nice stay in Jamaica,' an air stewardess said to me.

'Thank you.'

Warm Jamaican air hit me as I stepped down from the plane. I gazed up at the steep green hills that overlooked Kingston. A pink-red sunset niced up the horizon. I sniffed the salt air drifting over from the Caribbean Sea. White birds dipped their beaks into the still waters. It was good to see the Jamaican flag everywhere.

Home.

I held on to my football as I went through customs. Mum was the first to welcome me. She wrapped her arms around me and swayed me from side to side. She almost crushed me to death. Tears were in her eyes. 'So good to see you,' she said. She stroked my hair and hugged me again. 'Me have missed you, even you kicking your ball against the side of the house.'

Dad was there too, waiting with a trolley for my red suitcase. He half smiled before embracing me. 'We have all missed you, Kadeen. And we'll do everyting to keep you safe.'

He placed my suitcase and hand luggage on the trolley, and we made our way out of the airport. Crystal met us just outside the exit. She wasn't wearing her uniform. Instead she was styling denim shorts, white sandals and a Bob Marley One Love T-shirt. 'It's good to see you again, Kadeen. Thank you so much for doing this.'

I nodded before Crystal led the way to her car. It was a white Toyota estate. Nothing special. I don't know why, but I'd always imagined police officers driving SUVs with tinted windows for their personal use.

Dad loaded the boot as Crystal started the engine. I climbed into the back seat.

'How was your flight?' Mum asked. She sat beside me.

'Couldn't really sleep,' I replied. 'We had turbulence halfway over the Atlantic. The food was bad, bad, bad. No seasoning at all.'

Crystal laughed. 'Don't worry,' she said. 'The food at the Pegasus is five-star quality. Treat yourself to anyting you like. It's all on us.'

'But go easy on the Coca-Cola,' Mum warned. 'Me want a daughter wid teeth in her mouth.'

Dad slid into the front passenger seat, Crystal pushed into first gear and we were away. I looked through the rear window. I wasn't sure what or who I checked for, but I still felt uneasy.

I felt a little better as we checked in at the Pegasus Hotel. Mum and I shared a room. Dad and Crystal took rooms either side of us.

I had a short nap before Mum woke me up for dinner. We dined near the pool. I had curried goat, fried plantain and rice. *That was good.* I watched the early-evening swimmers, and they seemed to not have a care in the world.

Me must face him in two days. Me hope this mirror ting works. Me don't want him to see me.

The Girl With the Red Boots

'You all right, Kadeen?' Mum asked.

'Yes.' I nodded. 'Just a liccle weary.'

'Still jet-lagged,' added Dad. 'Don't worry, that'll pass in a few days.'

I turned to Crystal, who was enjoying some jerk chicken wings, fries and a big dose of barbecue sauce. 'This . . . mirror ting. You're sure it works?'

'Of course,' she replied. 'Don't stress yourself about that.'

'So from the other side, nobody can see me?' I needed confirmation.

'Nobody,' said Crystal.

'Does he know that he'll be taken to the police station for identification?' I asked.

'Oh, no,' replied Crystal. 'He won't know until that morning.'

'Where is he now?'

'He's being held at another top-security facility in Kingston.'

I managed to half smile. 'That's good to know.'

The next day I slept in late.

I didn't have breakfast until 10.30 a.m. I had roasted breadfruit, fried dumpling, salted cod fish and ackee, and washed it down with two glasses of orange juice.

Just twenty-four hours. Me want to get it over and done wid.

'You all right, Kadeen?' asked Mum.

'Yes.' I nodded. 'Still a bit groggy.'

Following breakfast, I made my way to the hotel gym. I

Homeland

pushed myself very hard on the bike and worked up a hot sweat. Edson's voice popped into my head. *You're doing the right ting, sis. Don't fret. Me watching over you. And you're going to make it as a footballer too. Believe that!*

Mum entered the gym and sat on the bike next to me. I wiped my face with a white towel.

'Going to work out?' I asked.

'Oh, no,' Mum said. 'Me wanted to talk to you, and me guess this place is as good as any.'

I looked around the gym. We were alone. 'OK,' I said.

'If you identify Tony Buttons, our lives will change forever,' Mum said. 'You do understand that?'

'Yes, of course.'

'You can still change your mind if you want to,' Mum said. 'We're asking a lot of you. Sometimes, me tink, too much. Me forget how young you are.'

I thought about it. 'Me can't lie,' I said. 'It's a scary ting. Sometimes at night, me imagine Tony Buttons coming for me wid all guns blazing. Other times it's people wid hoods over their faces. Me can only make out the eyes. But it's the same ting, all guns aiming at me . . . Me still want to go through wid it.'

'You sure?' Mum placed a hand on my shoulder. 'It's no shame to back down.'

'Me sure.' I nodded. 'One hundred per cent.'

'Me will put our house up for sale,' Mum revealed. 'And start looking for a new place. Me was tinking Mandeville. It's cooler up there.'

'Mandeville?' I repeated.

'It's a good distance away from Old Harbour,' Mum explained. 'But not too far that me can't get to work. Me can take the toll road where there's not too much traffic. Your friends could come up when they want to.'

'What about when me want to visit dem?'

'Then me or your father will be wid you . . . or nearby. Just as a precaution. You understand?'

I wasn't one hundred per cent OK with that, but I could see the sense in it.

'So, for now, me will be staying wid Dad and you'll be wid Aunt Doreen in May Pen.'

'Yes, that's the plan.' Mum nodded. 'You also have the option of changing your first name.'

'Seriously?'

'Yes, Crystal said that to me last night. For example, if you attend school in Mandeville or Montego Bay. Or even later if you apply for university or a job. She said you could even change the name on your passport. They will help us wid that.'

University? A job? Me want to be a footballer.

'Can . . . can me tink about that another time?' I asked. 'Just let me get through tomorrow.'

'Yes, of course,' said Mum. 'Sorry to hit you wid so many plans. Let's take tings day by day.'

32

Eye-to-Eye Contact

The journey to Olympic Gardens took twenty minutes or so. I forgot how driving in central Kingston could be so loud, with everybody slapping their car horns. Located near a busy junction was the Olympic Gardens police station. I guessed it was four storeys high. The building was freshly painted in blue and white. It had a sign outside the main entrance to the forecourt.

RULE OF LAW
RESPECT FOR ALL
A FORCE FOR GOOD
JAMAICA CONSTABULARY FORCE

Crystal showed her pass to the security man at the white gate. He let us through, and we parked in the car park. As

The Girl With the Red Boots

I climbed out of the car, I couldn't work out if the weather was way hotter than the day before, or if my nerves were making me sweat. I wondered if Tony Buttons was already inside.

Me hope he's handcuffed.

'Follow me,' said Crystal.

We did as we were told.

My stress levels went up another floor as I stepped into the building. We were met by an Officer Gordon at the entrance. His cap rested just above his eyebrows, and his light-blue shirt looked as if it had been ironed a few minutes ago. He had an easy smile. The gun strapped around his waist didn't make me feel safe.

Hate guns.

'You must be Kadeen.' Officer Gordon smiled. He offered his hand. I accepted it and shook it weakly. He pointed to the name badge clipped to his breast pocket. 'I'm Officer Jonathan Gordon. I'm part of the investigating team looking into your brother's . . . passing. We're liaising with our colleagues in Old Harbour.'

'Good to meet you,' I said.

'All of we really appreciate you and your family for coming down to the station today,' Officer Gordon said. 'It's very important. Come follow me and me will make sure you get any refreshments and anyting else you might need.'

He led us through a corridor that opened out into a canteen. We sat around a table that had menus on it. I went for a large banana, raspberry, strawberry and blueberry smoothie. Everyone else chose water.

'This week has been quiet,' Officer Gordon said. 'But you never know when tings will flare up again.'

'Too much gun on the island,' Mum replied. 'Where do they get dem from? How do they get dem through customs?'

'That's a very good question,' said Officer Gordon. 'We're trying our best to stem the flow and arrest the perpetrators.'

I finished my drink. I heard a bleeping sound from a device that Officer Gordon kept in his right trouser pocket. He read a message.

'Are you ready?' Officer Gordon asked me.

'Yes, me ready.' I nodded.

He led us through a security door and then downstairs. I sniffed the freshness of new paint. Old Harbour Police Station was nothing like this. Two turns later, we followed him through another security door.

'It's like a maze down here,' said Mum.

Officer Gordon opened a room by swiping a card. We entered. The space had a wooden table in the centre with a jug of water on it, and six chairs surrounding it. Officer Gordon switched on a light. Fixed to one wall was what looked like a massive flat-screen TV embedded into the brickwork. It was blank. There were no windows. Just plain white walls. A fan whirred above. It kept my head-top cool but it couldn't slow down the beat of my pulse.

'Make yourself comfortable,' said Officer Gordon.

The Girl With the Red Boots

We sat down facing the mirror. Dad poured drinks. Suddenly the mirror became active. Seven men were lined up. Some were tall, some were short. One had a lion tattoo on his neck. They all seemed to wish they were somewhere else. Everyone wore grey tracksuits. Different-coloured trainers wrapped their feet. Hanging from ribbons around their necks, not quite the size of chessboards, were numbers. One to seven.

Two of them stared at the wooden-tiled floor. The rest gazed into the mirror. My heartbeat bashed inside. There were officers in the room directing the men in the line-up, but we couldn't see or hear them.

There he was. Number two. He had lost his goatee beard. He wasn't quite so bald. His eyes reminded me of a shark's. No silver chain decorated his neck. He was shorter than I had expected. Stocky. Thick neck. It was him. Definitely. I shared a look with Mum. I sipped my water. It was very cold. My insides jiggled and wriggled. I swallowed saliva and took another dose of water. I remembered the warning from the man at the Mitcham Royals game and got even more nervous. But then I thought about Edson, and knew I had to do this for him.

'Can you identify the man you saw driving a white pick-up truck on South Street travelling towards Old Harbour Bay on February fifth of this year?' Officer Gordon asked.

'Yes, number two,' I replied without hesitation.

'Can you indicate the man you identified?'

Eye-to-Eye Contact

I stood up from my chair and pointed at Tony Buttons. He was quite still, glaring at the mirror.

Officer Gordon and Crystal wrote something in their notebooks.

'Can you recall the time you witnessed the man you identified driving the white pick-up truck on South Street on that day?'

'We left school at 3.15 p.m.,' I replied. 'So the time must have been a few minutes after that. Me remember it well becah the pick-up truck was driving on the wrong side of the road. It was swerving this way and that. Other cars tried to avoid it. It came very close to us. Me and my friends had to back off.'

'Was there enough time for you to have a good look at the driver?'

'Yes. Me can never forget his face. And that face is right there so.'

I pointed again.

Officer Gordon and Crystal scribbled again in their notebooks.

'That is it,' Officer Gordon said. 'After you have signed to confirm what you have just said, you're free to go.'

The mirror went dark.

'That is all?' I wanted confirmation.

'Yes.' Officer Gordon nodded. 'We have enough from you with your previous statement and now your identification of a suspect. We just need you to sign.'

Officer Gordon left the room. He returned ten minutes

later with a printed version of my identification statement. I signed two copies and blew out a sigh of relief.

Over. Me hope they keep him in that room till long after me gone.

'When are you going to charge him?' Mum wanted to know.

'Very soon,' Crystal replied. 'We have three more people willing to identify him today. If nobody contradicts each other, charges will follow.'

'Will Kadeen have to face him in court?' Dad asked.

'She's a minor,' Crystal said. 'If she is needed, she can present her evidence via video link-up.'

Relief.

Forty minutes later, we were back at the hotel.

I decided on a swim before I left for Montego Bay with Dad. My parents watched me as they sipped juices from the poolside. Crystal had said goodbye and was on her way back to Old Harbour.

I climbed out of the pool. 'You ready for the long drive?' Dad asked.

'Yes,' I said. 'But on the way, can we buy some flowers and stop off where Edson is resting and lay dem there?'

'Of course.'

Mum closed her eyes and nodded. 'You're a good girl, Kadeen.'

I'm sure it was my imagination, but it seemed the clouds above opened a little as if Edson heard me.

Eye-to-Eye Contact

I knew he was proud.

Two days later, Tony Buttons, or whatever name he now calls himself, was charged with my brother's murder. It was on the front page of two newspapers. I didn't feel any sense of victory. Just . . . relief.

33

Teamwork

Three months later, I was wading barefoot through the soft waves of Old Harbour Bay. I carried my sandals in my hands. A hot Jamaican sun blazed above me. My face was cooled by a breeze coming in from the Caribbean. Sienna, Melody and Emma were with me. We had left Mum, Aunt Mel and Dad at a seafront cocktail bar. For the first time in months, I felt safe and comfortable – my team were here with me.

A fisherman smiled at us as he pushed his red-, gold- and green-painted boat out to sea. 'Morning, pretty ladies,' he greeted, before jumping in his vessel and steering his way with a single paddle.

Bigger ships had dropped anchor in the distance. The horizon was hazy.

Teamwork

'Have you decided on a new name yet?' asked Sienna.

'Me was tinking of Georgia,' I replied.

Sienna gave me side-eye.

'Georgia?' repeated Melody. 'Why in the Lord's name would you name yourself after a US state?'

'It could be worse,' said Emma. 'It might have been Pennsylvania Best.'

'Or Nebraska Best,' laughed Sienna.

'Nebraska?' repeated Melody. 'Actually, that's not too bad. Fling away Georgia and call yourself Nebraska . . . or even Ohio. Yes, Ohio Best sound good to me.'

'Me not naming meself after a US state,' I explained. 'It's after an old-school baller.'

'And her name is Georgia?' Emma asked.

'No, it's a he,' I replied. 'Georgie Best. Me did look him up on YouTube. Trust me, he was a wicked baller. Nobody could take the ball off him. Him scored nuff goals for Manchester United.'

'Georgia Best,' said Sienna. 'Me suppose we must get used to it. Your name will change again when you marry Cass Buckley.'

'Mrs Georgia Buckley,' grinned Melody. 'It has a nice ring to it. Good morning, Mrs Georgia Buckley!'

'Me not going to marry Cass Buckley or anyone else,' I protested. 'Me too young!'

'But you want him to come to your birthday party in September,' said Emma.

The Girl With the Red Boots

'Yes! You did say that,' added Sienna. 'Just yesterday.'

'I want to meet this Cass Buckley,' said Emma. 'I've heard so much about him since I started my holiday.'

'He's handsome,' said Melody. 'Me give him that.'

'And sporty,' added Sienna. 'Nice long legs.'

I tried to kill my blush.

'Me hope he's not so peckish as Wilson McKenzie,' said Melody. 'He just wanted the one ting. Me had to fling Wilson to the kerb.'

'Me mother says they all want the one ting,' put in Sienna.

'Me don't know if me parents will even allow me to have a party,' I said.

'Noooo!' Melody raised her voice. 'You *must* have a party. You still haven't seen all of your friends since you left Old Harbour and gone to England. Everyone has missed you.'

Emma heard something and turned. We all looked behind. Dad waved his hands about trying to get our attention. We jogged back to the bar he was drinking at. Mum held her phone up in the air. 'It's Coach Francis,' she said. 'She was trying to call you.'

'Out by the sea it's hard to get a Wi-Fi connection,' I said.

Mum gave me her phone. A strange smile grew from her lips.

'Coach Francis,' I said. 'It's great to hear from you.'

'And it's lovely to hear your voice,' she replied. 'It's getting late here, but I have some wonderful news for you.'

'You do?'

Teamwork

'Yes, Chelsea Academy have been in touch,' Coach Francis revealed. 'They want you to come over for trials.'

'For trials? Seriously?'

'I wouldn't joke about that sorta thing,' said Coach Francis. 'Apparently, someone filmed our last game, showed the highlights to the people at Chelsea, and they believe you have a special talent. She didn't introduce herself because she didn't want anyone to feel nervous before such a big game.'

'Oh, my gosh! But it was Tracey who scored the two goals.'

'And it was your pace and skill that set them up.'

'Chelsea Academy?'

'Yes, Chelsea Academy. They're willing to pay for everything. Your flights, living expenses, the whole doughnuts. They don't want to interrupt your education, but they're looking at the next school break.'

The conversation was on speaker. I looked at Mum, Dad, Aunt Mel and my friends. They all smiled and nodded.

'You can stay with me,' offered Emma.

'It's a wonderful opportunity,' added Coach Francis. 'I'll reckon you'll be in the first team before you reach seventeen. That's what I said to the lady who called me.'

'Me don't know what to say,' I managed. 'It's . . . it's . . .'

'It's what Edson would have wanted for you,' said Dad. 'Just say yes. We'll sort out the this, that and how afterwards.'

'*Yes*,' I said. 'Yes!' I turned to Sienna. 'When is the next school break?'

'October.'

'Tell dem October,' I said to Coach Francis. 'Tell dem Georgia Best is coming in October. Me going to be a footballer!'

Acknowledgements

The author would like to thank the following people for their work on this book.

Katie Lawrence – Editor
Joana Reis – Designer
Laura Pritchard – Senior Desk Editor
Hazel Cotton – Copyeditor
Becca Allen – Proofreader
Joelyn Rolston-Esdelle – Production Manager
Dominic Kingston, Bec Gillies, Karis Pearson – Marketing and Publicity
Berat Pekmezci – Cover Illustrator

Alex Wheatle is the author of several acclaimed novels, many of them inspired by experiences from his childhood. He was born in Brixton to Jamaican parents and spent most of his childhood in a Surrey children's home. After a short stint in prison following the Brixton uprising of 1981, he wrote poems and lyrics and became known as the Brixtonbard. Alex was shortlisted for numerous awards, including the Carnegie Medal and the YA Book Prize. He won the Guardian Children's Fiction Prize and was awarded an MBE for services to literature in 2008.

You can find out more about Alex here:

www.alexwheatle.com

'... ENRICHING AND
LIFE-AFFIRMING'
INDEPENDENT

'... POWERFUL WRITING BY
AN AUTHOR WITH GREAT TALENT
AND GREAT HEART'
DAVID ALMOND

'A MAJOR VOICE IN BRITISH
CHILDREN'S LITERATURE'
S. F. SAID

WELCOME TO CRONGTON,
WHERE YOUR LOYALTY AND WITS WILL BE TESTED...

COLLECT ALL OF THE *CRONGTON* SERIES.

'GRIPPING'
MALORIE BLACKMAN

ALSO BY ALEX WHEATLE

'STUDDED WITH WHEATLE'S CHARACTERISTIC SLANG, NAOMI'S STORY IS BOTH HEARTBREAKING AND HILARIOUS, OFFERING NO EASY HAPPY ENDINGS, BUT A FLICKERING SENSE OF HOPE.'

GUARDIAN

COMING SOON:

A BRAND-NEW FESTIVE INSTALMENT OF THE MUST-READ *CRONGTON* SERIES

Want to be the first to hear about the best new teen and YA reads?

Want exclusive content, offers and giveaways?

Want to chat about books with people who love them as much as you do?

Look no further...

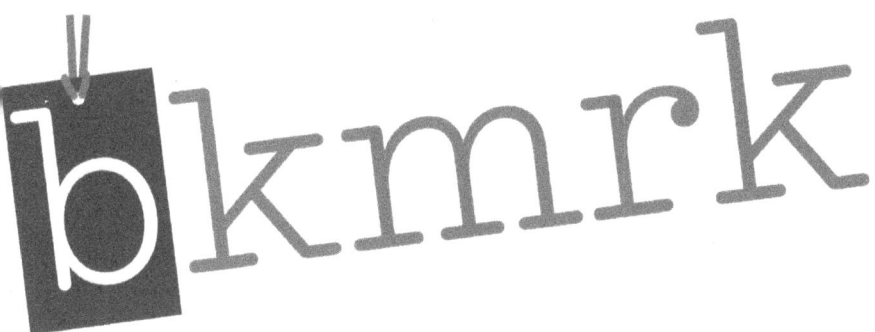

Sign up to our newsletter now!

See you there!
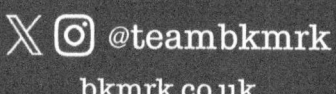 @teambkmrk
bkmrk.co.uk